WE ARE THE GIRLS OF BUNK 5A!

And these are our fave things...

Belle
(Counsellor)
My trusty clipboard!

Clarissa
(CIT - counsellor-in-training)
Spooky stories and ice cream

Natalie
Fashion mags and
nail polish

Jenna
Playing pranks!

Grace
Making new friends!

Alyssa
Writing in my
journal

Tori
Shopping, of course!

Brynn
Broadway shows,
dahling!

Alex
Sports –
especially soccer

Gaby
Getting my own way
– kidding!

Valerie
Dancing my socks off

Priya
Making up
gross dares

Chelsea
My cute

SUMMER CAMP SECRETS

Fancy some more sizzling Summer Camp fun?
Check out

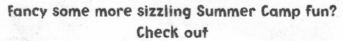

www.summercampsecrets.co.uk

Hide and Shriek

Melissa.J.Morgan

First published in the UK in 2009 by Usborne Publishing Ltd., Usborne House, 83-85 Saffron Hill, London EC1N 8RT, England. www.usborne.com

A CIP catalogue record for this book is available from the British Library.

ISBN 9781409505532   JFM MJJASOND/09 89871   Printed in Great Britain.

PROLOGUE

They're coming, he thought as he watched the fog slowly take form above the jagged coves and uncharted crannies of mysterious Shadow Lake.

This year, he would be ready.

I made a mistake last time. I let them get away.

The fog boiled up from the water and rolled towards him. An owl hooted beneath the bone-white moon, warning the little creatures in the dark woods that danger lurked everywhere, and they had better stay alert if they wanted to survive the night. Nature could be cruel. So could fate.

His right hand – his only hand – gripped the rotted wood of the post on the porch of the old cabin. The wood pulped between his fingers in an ooze of dry rot and decay. He was still panting from his explosion of fury.

He had been down in the basement, searching for his old axe and a couple of heads. There was so much junk down there – maps of the woods, some kid's backpack, a pair of rusted handcuffs – that he couldn't find the heads at first. Turned out they'd rolled behind the rotted couch upstairs.

He grabbed them and the axe and hurried outside. The cabin bulged with ghosts, and he couldn't stand being inside it longer than he had to. It should have been torn down long ago.

Soon, he promised himself.

His smile cracked the purple scars across his features. He turned his head slightly to the left. It was a habit he'd developed after he lost his left eye. His black eyepatch looked like an empty eye socket in the ebony darkness.

He took the first step down, then the next, and limped off the porch. The axe blade gleamed in the bone-white moonlight. He carried the heads by their hair.

When his boot touched the gritty earth, the frogs and crickets stopped singing. The owl cut short her beckoning hoot. The woods fell completely silent, and the pine boughs trembled.

The fog raced fearlessly towards him.

He limped towards shrouded Shadow Lake. His bones ached. He had been through so much. He had to get it right this time, so he could finally rest.

He had tied his old dinghy to a desiccated tree trunk that lay half submerged in the water. It looked like a bloated dead giant. The heavy fog gave it the illusion of floating in mid-air; it bobbed and tugged against the moor line as if it wanted to escape.

He knew the feeling.

He deposited the axe and the heads in the bow of the boat. They rolled together, then rolled apart, their eyes staring at him blankly. They were old friends. Friends he needed now, hopefully for the last time. He winked at them with his right eye. They did not wink back.

Then he held onto the tree trunk and stepped cautiously onto the slightly curved bottom of the dinghy. The craft wobbled as he found his balance. When he had first lost his arm, simple things like this had been nearly impossible to accomplish. But he had surmounted many hardships to achieve his ends. He had an iron will...and he didn't take failure lightly.

He clenched his jaw and slowly sat down on the seat of the boat. Then he cast off, drifting into the fog. From the bottom of the boat, he grabbed his paddle. A set of oars were useless for a man with one arm.

The flat wooden paddle cut through the water like a knife as he glided through the phantom layers of mist to the secret spot. He had hidden it well.

His single eye ticked downwards through the fog to

the lake, the final resting place of his hopes and dreams. If only *they* knew what lay beneath the surface of Shadow Lake. They'd be surprised. But all that belonged to the lake now.

Behind him, safely distant, the owl hooted long and low. *He's gone. It's safe to come out*, they seemed to be saying. The forest creatures skittered and darted. The woods heaved a sigh of relief.

He lifted his chin in the direction of the highway that sliced through the landscape beyond the hills and trees. It was the road they would take.

"This time, I'll get you."

And he knew that once he'd finally achieved his ends, he would disappear from Shadow Lake for ever.

CHAPTER ONE

Dear Grace,

Nat here! I am writing to you from the bus, which is why my handwriting is so squiggly. I've tried to text you a gazillion times on my cellphone, but the reception up here is not happening. I guess it's so remote here in rural Pennsylvania that they don't have a lot of can-you-hear-me-now guys making sure our phones work.

Alyssa's on the bus. Tori, too. She flew in last night so we could hang in New York together. Lyss, as usual, is writing and sketching in one of her notebooks. Tori bounced a couple of rows back to talk to some kids about crops. I have no clue why she thinks that's interesting, but I'm sure she'll fill me in later.

Our hot, stinky coach has been chugging along for ever, but we're almost at Camp Lake-puke. Guess how I know! We've hit that super-extra-bumpy part of the road. See? You can tell by my even worse handwriting. Plus, we just zoomed past the sign that says "Camp Lakeview 15 kilometres". Witness my mad detective skills! LOL.

I wish I brought my iPod to drown out the noise. Everyone except Lyss, Tori and me is singing "Ninety-Nine Bottles of Beer on the Wall" for the fifth or sixth time. It's more like yelling. Even Paula Abdul would admit that the tune got lost about a hundred and thirty bottles ago.

I can't believe it's my third summer at this crazy-fun place. Do you remember our first summer together, when my mom forced me to "broaden my horizons" and shipped me out here while she went off on an art-buying trip to Europe? Remember how I freaked out? No air conditioning, ginormous spiders and vampire mosquitoes, and camp food? I was ready to go back to Manhattan that very first day!

But you were so funny and friendly that I actually forgot to be miserable. Now you are one of my best Camp Lakeview Friends (CLFs for life!), and I had to actually talk my mom into <u>letting</u> me come this year instead of going with her to Asia on her art-buying trip.

Seriously, Grace, I can't wait to see you. I'm so glad you only have to miss the first two weeks of camp. You'll breeze through summer school, wait and see! English will not defeat you! After all, you passed history!

Tori's in da house! She just came back to sit with us. Now I will hear about the crops.

Oh! She wasn't listening to a conversation about <u>crops</u>, she was listening to a story about someone called <u>Cropsy</u>. She says this is the sixth year of some hideous tragedy that takes place every six years at Shadow Lake! She's going to tell Alyssa and me all about it in gory detail. Mwahaha! If it's any good, I'll give you the full low-down!

See you in two weeks!

T T F N, Nat

"Okay, I have confirmation on the dark secret of Shadow Lake."

Tori plopped down into the empty seat behind Alyssa and Natalie and leaned over their sweaty shoulders. "The story I heard is the story *they* heard. And it's all true. So, are you ready to be scared out of your wits?"

"But of course! Bring it on," Natalie said, blowing tendrils of wavy brown hair off her forehead. Despite the open windows – or perhaps because of them – it was hot and muggy inside the bus. Tori's original seatmate had gone to cram herself in with her buds at the front of the bus, so Tori had her seat all to herself. Alyssa, her dark hair pulled back in a messy bun, was sitting in front of Tori with Natalie, and they turned around to face her so they could chat.

Tori launched into her so-very-terrifying story. "Okay, so this homicidal maniac—"

"A what?" Alyssa asked, cupping her ear. "I can't hear you."

"It's about a homicidal maniac," Tori repeated, raising her voice.

Trading excited looks, Natalie and Alyssa leaned even further over the seat to listen, and Tori noticed how much they'd changed in the last year. All three of them were definitely growing up. As ever, she and Natalie were way ahead on the trend curve in the hair and make-up departments. Tori had stylish blonde Paris Hilton hair and a black T-shirt with CHIC written on it. Natalie was up-to-the-minute in her polka-dot bubble top, and they both had on fancy flip-flops decorated with bows and charms.

Alyssa appeared content to stay with her artist look of a torn T-shirt and paint-splattered jeans (in this weather!), her dark eyelashes accentuated by lots of heavy black mascara and dramatic ebony butterfly earrings. But Natalie and Alyssa's faces were a little longer and thinner, Tori noticed. More mature. It was both cool and scary at the same time.

Like my story.

"I originally heard this from my Pennsylvania cousin, Nicole," she began. Then she frowned when she saw that they were still straining to hear her. She figured it was best to unravel her creepy tale of death in a hushed, spooky tone, but two-thirds of the bus was still determined to count beer bottles backwards, in song.

"I really should wait to tell it," she ventured, but both Natalie and Alyssa made sad-puppy faces.

"You can*not* stop now," Natalie insisted. "We will die of curiosity."

"You will not," Tori said, laughing. "I haven't even started!"

"Okay, maybe we won't die, but we will get very

sick," Natalie insisted. "Please, please, please?"

Alyssa, the more subdued one, raised her eyebrows in a silent request.

"All right," Tori relented. "You know I got sent to Lakeview last year because my mom came here? Well, that and to make friends with kids outside of Hollywood."

Natalie nodded with the total understanding of one who had been there, done that, gotten the T-shirt. Both their families were big in the entertainment industry.

Tori paused and held up her finger. "My cousin Nicole — she's way older than us — used to come here. Every summer. Then six years ago, something terrible happened....and she never came back again."

"Why not?" Natalie asked, her eyes wide. Beside her, Alyssa gestured for Tori to go on.

Tori paused for dramatic effect. Then she said, "She never came back because that summer Cropsy tried to kidnap her bunkmate's cousin, who was in another bunk, and cut off her arm!"

"Yow!" Natalie cried.

"Who's Cropsy?" Alyssa asked, her jaw dropping.

Tori cleared her throat. "Cropsy. The one-armed monster of Shadow Lake. When the fog rises, he—"

"Okay, campers," Pete said into a megaphone as he got to his feet and planted himself in a wide stance in the aisle. In his early twenties, he was tan and fit. He wore a Camp Lakeview polo shirt and a pair of khaki cargo shorts. He was holding a clipboard, and he waited for the singing to die down before he spoke again.

"Later," Tori said to Natalie and Alyssa.

"Wah!" Natalie scrunched up her face. Beside her, Alyssa bit her lower lip and groaned.

"Bookmarking this conversation," Tori promised, and the two girls nodded.

"A lot of you already know me," Pete went on. "For those of you who don't, I'm Pete, sometimes a counsellor, and for the last few years, your humble cook."

"Oh, *please* tell us you're going to be a humble counsellor this year," one of the boys shouted from the back, and half the bus started laughing.

Tori, Alyssa and Natalie giggled. On a scale from one to ten, the food at camp was...*not* a box office smash. In fact, Tori had been fascinated in an I-cannot-believe-this-is-really-my-breakfast kind of way by just how bad it was. This year she had wised up and followed Natalie's lead, cramming her send-ahead camp trunk with a survival stash of soy chips, PowerBars, and a crate of the new bottled water she and Kallista, her best friend back home, had discovered at Whole Foods. The camp food was bad, but the weak-but-way-too-sugary bug juice was even worse.

"Sorry to disappoint you, but I'm cooking again this year," Pete informed them. Everyone groaned. "Okay, now that we've settled that, let's move along. Because speaking of moving along, we're almost at camp."

Cheers, applause and foot stomps blared over whatever he was going to say next. Tori and Natalie cried "Woo-hoo!" while Alyssa grinned big-time at her two friends. Natalie folded up her letter to Grace and stuck it into her bright pink daypack, and Alyssa closed her notebook, which she had decorated the front of with silhouettes of modern dancers in African masks – in honour of their friend Valerie, Tori guessed.

"Once you get off the bus, pick up your stuff from Bob, our fearless driver," Pete said as the driver raised his right hand from the big grey steering wheel and gave a jaunty wave. "Your counsellors will be looking for you, but if you can't find your counsellor, stick with me or Nurse Helen so we can help. She'll be meeting the bus too."

Pete checked his big black sports watch. "You'll have about an hour to stow your stuff and then we'll meet by the lake for the cookout."

"All right! Pete's not cooking today!" the same guy in the back yelled.

Everyone started cheering again.

"You need to finish your story about Flopsy as soon

as possible, okay?" Natalie asked. She was teasing about Cropsy's name.

"I will," Tori promised. "But you probably won't be able to sleep tonight."

"I won't be able to sleep tonight anyway," Natalie said. "We'll be too busy talking after lights-out."

"*If* we have a cooperative counsellor," Alyssa reminded them. "Sometimes we actually have to follow the rules."

"Maybe we'll get one who's a heavy sleeper," Natalie said hopefully.

"We might want a light sleeper," Tori said. "In case Cropsy tries to break into our bunk."

Then she caught sight of the green sign planted on a white post along the side of the road that read CAMP LAKEVIEW 1 KILOMETRE.

Natalie saw it too. "Look, guys! We're almost there!"

"Where Cropsy will be waiting, mwahaha," Tori promised.

It was almost noon in muggy rural Pennsylvania and thunderclouds were pressing down on the sky. Standing with Jenna, Candace and Brynn in the Camp Lakeview parking lot, Alex could smell the burning charcoal as the preparations for the welcome cookout got under way. The odour mingled with the insect repellent on her arms – the smells of summer and Camp Lakeview. It was opening day, and they were waiting for the bus that was bringing Tori, Natalie and Alyssa to a summer of fun and friendship...or so Alex hoped. Something was wrong in the fifth division, and Alex was freaked.

"They're late," Jenna fretted, looping her curly brown hair around her ears.

"They're not late," Alex insisted, shaking her head of short black hair. "It's like this every year. On the first day, people show up at all different times. So there's no such thing as late. Just...last."

As if to prove her point, two cars and another bus unloaded passengers on the opposite side of the lot. A puff of exhaust added to the bouquet of first-day smells.

"Well I wish they'd show," Jenna said, bouncing on her heels. She reached into the pocket of her shorts and pulled out a pack of gum. "Anybody want some?"

"Thanks," Alex said as she took a piece of extreme cinnamon. Candace and Brynn took some too. While Alex unwrapped it, she squinted at the nickel-coloured horizon. She'd forgotten her sunglasses in their new bunk, 5A, which was located at the top of the pine-studded hill overlooking the lake. She didn't want to go all the way back up there to get them. It was too hot, and besides, she wanted to see Natalie,

Alyssa and Tori the moment they arrived.

Jenna grabbed Alex's wrist and checked the face of her watch, the one with the little soccer balls on the navy blue strap. "They are *too* late. They're five whole minutes late."

"My watch is fast," Alex said.

"Her watch is fast," Candace told Jenna.

Alex found it oddly reassuring that Candace still had the habit of repeating the things people around her said. It was one of the few things that seemed intact from last summer.

"Six minutes *late*," Jenna said, still reading the time on Alex's watch.

"Will this torment never end?" Brynn cried, making a show of pulling out her dark red hair.

Alex silently chuckled at Brynn's theatrics. Brynn was still a major drama queen — which was good, since Brynn's goal in life was to become an actress. She was already starring in plays at school, and she had actually considered skipping Camp Lakeview this summer to go to a drama camp instead.

Alex was seriously glad Brynn had decided to come to Lakeview after all, because so many others hadn't. She was bummed to find out that Sarah and Abby weren't coming back. Neither were Karen and Jessie. And that was what was wrong with the fifth division —

a startling number of girls Alex's age had opted to spend their summer vacations somewhere else.

At least most of my closest camp buds are here, Alex thought.

Arriving throughout the day, Brynn, Alex and Jenna had reunited in their new bunk and hugged and chatted while they waited for everyone else to show. Candace was there too. No one had seen or spoken to her since last summer. Everyone already knew Clarissa, their CIT, because she'd been a camper last year. Blonde and bouncy, she was an interesting cross between a girlie-girl and a jock.

Their counsellor, Belle, was new, and she was kind of...strange. She was very pale, and she had super-black hair, but she wasn't a goth. She was friendly enough, but she seemed awfully nervous. The four bunkmates had exchanged glances when she had greeted them and explained a few of her bunk policies — such as no calling top bunks until everyone had arrived. That was fairly standard, but when she told them, her pale cheeks reddened and she looked down at her clipboard like telling them was some huge deal.

Now, in the parking lot, Alex heard a low, deep rumble, and for a moment she thought it was thunder. Then a ginormous red and white bus with CAMP LAKEVIEW CHARTER spelled out above the front windshield trundled from behind a stand of pine trees and rolled towards the girls.

"It's them!" Brynn tossed back her red hair as she arched backwards and flung her arms towards the sky. "The long wait is over!"

Beside Alex, Jenna bounced on her heels like Tigger and waved her arms like she was guiding a jet down the runway at an airport. Candace clapped her hands with excitement, straining to see the three girls they were all looking for – Tori, Natalie and Alyssa.

"Look! Natalie Goode! Dead ahead!" Jenna called, pointing with both forefingers at the approaching bus. "Yo, Nat!"

Peering out through a grimy window above one of the bus's large wheels, Natalie waved excitedly at the foursome in the parking lot. Tori and Alyssa crowded into the same window, and Alex felt her heart soar. She had missed those guys.

The bus chugged onto the tarmacked parking lot. Its air brakes squealed. Then the driver turned off the motor.

"Natalia, *mi amore*! Tori! Lyss!" Brynn cried.

She flung open her arms and raced towards the bus. Alex found herself running to catch up with Brynn. Sprinting along, Jenna and Candace crashed into each other, laughed, and hurried along too.

The bus door slammed open with a rush of air. Some

other kids got off the bus, and then Natalie, Tori and Alyssa hopped down the three stairs and raced for Alex and the others. Their feet had barely touched the tarmac before the hugging began.

"You're here!" Jenna cried.

"We're here!" Natalie high-fived her. "Tell us what bunks we're in. I swear, if I'm not with at least some of you guys—"

"We're all together," Alex told her.

Natalie and Tori squealed, and Alyssa grinned.

"That rocks!" Tori cried.

"Who else is in our bunk? Anyone we know?" Natalie asked as she moved to collect her enormous duffel bag, which Alex recognized from summers past. It was as big as the upright piano in Alex's living room – and weighed twice as much, no doubt.

"Yes. We know all our bunkmates," Alex replied. "No new girls at all."

"Wow," Alyssa said, pausing for a moment as she slipped her arms through her backpack. "Really? No one new?"

"There's the seven of us," Alex said, indicating the group in the lot. "And Priya. And Valerie."

"O-kay, that's a total of nine," Natalie said slowly. "Then Grace is coming late. That's ten. And there's usually eleven to a bunk."

There was a moment's silence where no one asked the question that immediately sprang to mind. Alex answered it anyway.

"They're going to bump us up to twelve when Grace comes," Alex said. "So we have two more." She took a breath. "Chelsea is in our bunk. *And* Gaby. We haven't seen them yet, but they're on our roster."

The girls took it about as well as Alex would have expected, given their difficult past history with both girls. Chelsea could be really snarky and mean-spirited, and Gaby was super-bossy. Ever since Chelsea had started coming to camp, way back when they were in the third division, Alex and her friends had tried really hard to get along with her. Gaby was no less challenging.

"About that art trip to Asia," Natalie muttered as she pulled the duffel bag upright, cocking her head and staring at the bag as if she had no idea how to carry it. Then she put her arms around the top end.

"I'm sure we'll all get along fine."

"Ya-huh, right," Jenna muttered back. "Who hates us enough to give us Chelsea *and* Gaby?"

"Yes, I'm happy to see you, too," said a sour voice. Alex winced. It was a very familiar sour voice.

Then Chelsea stepped into view with her duffel bag slung over her shoulder. She was still peaches-and-cream pretty, with her blonde hair in a loose, attractive braid down her back. But the familiar deep scowl on her face detracted from her looks. It appeared that she had been coming towards them from the other side of the parking lot, hidden by the bulky charter bus.

Without another word, she stomped away.

Everyone stared after her, too numb with shock to speak.

"That went well," Jenna finally said.

Everyone groaned in unison.

A deep wave of hurt coursed through Chelsea as she hoisted her duffel bag over her shoulder and walked through the crowds of campers laughing and greeting one another like the long-lost friends they were.

She *knew* she shouldn't have come back to Camp Lakeview. She *knew* those girls would still be mean and petty. But she had dared to hope that maybe she could start over with them, and that this summer would be different. But it wasn't going to be different, was it?

She wished she could call her mom and ask her to take her home. But at this very moment, her father and mother were at a clinic in Washington DC, so her father could participate in a medical trial for a new kind of cancer drug. Her mother had had to quit her job to accompany him, and she was living in a special house provided by a charity organization so they wouldn't have to go even further in debt to pay for her lodging. Chelsea's older sister was staying with her best friend's family back home, and Chelsea's uncle had paid for Chelsea's camp because she *didn't* have a best friend whose family offered to keep her for the summer.

So she couldn't go home. She was at Camp Lakeview for the entire summer, whether she liked it or not. And so far, she didn't like it at all.

*I wish...*she thought. What did she wish?

I wish those snotty girls would go away and never come back.

Stumbling over a pine cone, she bit her lower lip to keep herself from bursting into tears as she tromped up the hill towards their bunk.

CHAPTER TWO

Stricken, Nat started off across the parking lot after Chelsea, then stopped and flopped her arms down at her sides. She should probably wait for Chelsea to blow off some steam before she tried to apologize.

Behind her, Alex sighed. "Talk about lousy timing."

"I'm sorry, you guys." Natalie turned and faced the group. She caught her lower lip between her teeth and scrunched up her nose. "I should have kept my mouth shut."

"Me too." Jenna hung her head.

"Me too." Candace exhaled and laced her hands across her stomach.

"You didn't say anything at all," Nat reminded Candace.

"Yeah, but I was about to," Candace replied, eyes wide, bobbing her head.

Brynn raised her hand. "Me four. Only my love of

the dramatic pause stopped me in time."

"I need to learn to love the dramatic pause." Nat looked over her shoulder at the receding figure. "We'll have to figure out a way to make it up to her. We can't start the summer off like this."

"If she wants a top bunk, we should let her have one," Candace ventured.

"Chelsea's mood can be changed with the addition of a little sugar," Jenna announced. Her trademark impish smile brightened up her freckled face. "And my mom sent along two dozen of her killer chocolate-on-chocolate cupcakes."

Now it was Brynn's turn to groan – or rather, moan – with sheer delight. "Your mom is a goddess!"

Alex smiled like the other girls, but Nat knew that of course she couldn't have one of the cupcakes. Alex had juvenile diabetes, and she had to monitor her sugar intake carefully. Two summers ago, after she had eaten too many Twinkies and skipped an insulin injection, she had gone into diabetic shock. Only the quick thinking of their counsellor had kept it from getting any worse than that.

"What about Gaby?" Candace asked. "Do you think Chelsea will tell her what we said?"

"I hope not." Nat shook her head. She couldn't imagine an entire summer feuding with Chelsea and

Gaby. She had hoped they were all old enough to figure out how to get along.

That would include you, Goode, she reminded herself. *Saying mean things about your bunkmates was pretty immature.*

The crowds were beginning to thin as the campers headed for their bunks – or to get to the cookout early so they could stake out their favourite picnic table and snag one of the first hot dogs or hamburgers off the grill. Bob the bus driver finished taking the luggage out of the storage area in the undercarriage of the bus and drove away.

"Guys, we have to check in with our counsellor," Tori said as she reached for the extendable handle of an elegant black wheeled suitcase.

"She's at the bunk. We'll lead the way," Jenna announced, gesturing for the other girls to follow her. "We're up the hill this year."

"I'll carry this if the ground gets too rough," Tori said.

"I hope we're not in trouble with Belle," Candace murmured. "That's our counsellor's name."

"In trouble for what, saying how we feel when we thought we had some privacy?" Jenna asked, but she looked a little worried too. "Argh, *why* did she have to hear us?"

They left the parking lot and walked past the

infirmary and the mess hall. The American flag and the Camp Lakeview flag hung limply in the moist air. Then the Christmas-y scent of pine filled Natalie's nose as they started up the path of hard-packed earth lined with small rocks on either side.

Alex paused on the trail. "About Belle." She smoothed her short dark hair and lowered her arm to her side, hesitating. "She's a little..." She trailed off. "Never mind. Maybe it's just me."

"It's not just you," Brynn said. "In a word? She's... freaky."

"Freaky? How?" Tori asked, making a face as her suitcase wheels rattled over a scattering of small stones and dried pine needles.

Alex looked at Brynn, who was staggering beneath the weight of Nat's duffel. Brynn wiped her forehead.

"She's intense. Or maybe the word is 'tense'."

"Tense works for me," Jenna said. "Weirdly tense."

"Maybe it's her first year as a counsellor," Nat suggested. "She's new here, right? I've never heard of a counsellor at Lakeview named Belle before."

"Yes, she's new. She's from Maine," Brynn said. "And they must not get any sun up there in Maine, because she's white as a ghost."

"Ghostly," Candace said.

"Maybe she *is* a ghost." Tori wiggled her eyebrows.

"Speaking of ghosts and changing the subject, Tori has a spooky story to share," Nat announced with a little smile. She knew her friend was *dying* to tell it.

"Oooh," Candace murmured. "Is it very spooky?"

"It's not just spooky. It's horrifying," Tori assured them. "And it's not just a story. It's true. I'll tell it tonight and scare the wits out of everyone!"

"No way!" Brynn cried. "I'm still having nightmares about the ghost stories we heard last year."

"Me too." Candace's lower lip quivered. "Nightmares."

"I like to be scared," Jenna insisted. "Adam and I watch horror movies all the time." Nat ticked her attention to Alex. Adam was Jenna's twin brother, and he and Alex were currently sweeties.

"Then tonight is your lucky night," Tori promised. She winked at Brynn and Candace. "I'll be sure to tell it when you two aren't around."

Brynn made a face. "Hmmm. I'll probably weaken and listen to every gory detail. I'm like that. Can't stand to miss good drama."

"This is seriously good drama," Tori assured her.

They walked on for a little while. The hill was awfully steep. Tori gave up and carried her suitcase.

"What is *in* this thing?" Brynn asked, reshifting her half of Nat's duffel in her arms.

"A summer's supply of make-up, nail polish and the June *and* July issues of all our favourite magazines," Nat replied breezily, trying to lighten the mood. "By the way, I checked everyone's horoscopes before I left this morning." She rolled her eyes. "*My* horoscope said that I should exercise caution when expressing myself."

"And yet you chose to ignore it," Brynn said.

"Good to know," Candace put in.

"Yeah, well." Nat grimaced. "I still feel totally awful that Chelsea heard me. She's been through so much."

The others nodded. Chelsea's father had been battling cancer on and off for several years. That was a horrible enough situation for anyone to be in, but it seemed worse for Chelsea because she had so much trouble making and keeping friends – at least at camp. Nat tried to give her the benefit of the doubt, but Chelsea could be awfully snarky and mean. It was incredible bad luck that Chelsea had overheard the girls – *okay, me and Jenna* – talking about her.

Nat stopped, fished in her daypack, and pulled on the pair of Italian sunglasses her father had bought for her on a location shoot of his latest film. She looked up at the hill. "I wish I didn't have to face Chelsea again so soon."

"The cookout's going to start in less than an hour,"

Alex pointed out. "Maybe we can try to make up there, on neutral territory."

"Remember how Chelsea weaselled the last hot dog out of Karen?" Jenna asked. "Maybe Karen didn't come back because she was tired of putting up with Chelsea."

"Karen was starting to stand up to Chelsea," Natalie said. "It was so nice to see her becoming more self-confident."

"Now Karen's gone and we get to keep Chelsea," Brynn muttered. Then she said, "I did not just say that. I am through with gossiping about anyone I've ever met."

"Tell us about *our* horoscopes," Alex suggested, moving the conversation along.

Nat pointed a manicured finger at her more simply-dressed friend. Alex favoured khaki and navy blue, and her nails were plain and short. "Your horoscope said to be flexible because big changes are on their way!"

"I'm tired of changes," Alex grumped as she turned around and walked backwards up the slope. "Nothing ever stays the same."

"That's what makes life so exciting," Brynn retorted.

"I like my excitement on the soccer field." Alex was known as Camp Lakeview's soccer superstar, and she lived up to her reputation. The shelves in her room glittered with rows of soccer trophies.

Huffing, the girls reached a wood-burned sign shaped like an arrow. It read FIFTH DIVISION CABINS, and the path forked to the right.

"Well, my story is beyond exciting," Tori promised them. She slapped at a mosquito. "And filled with blood, just like this fiend of nature!"

"Did you see Jordan yet?" Nat asked Brynn, who went all girlfriendy-blushy.

"No, not yet," Brynn answered. "And Priya's not here yet, either. Priya's father is driving them in together."

"Valerie has yet to show, too," Alex said.

"Simon is with Adam," Jenna told Nat. "They went on down to the lake."

"It'll be nice to see him again." Nat smiled, happy but not super-ultra-happy. She and cutie Simon had tried out being boyfriend and girlfriend, but they had decided having a long-distance romance was too awkward.

They continued up the hill. Nat half-expected to run into Chelsea, but she must have punched the turbo to put some distance between herself and them.

"I wonder if she's complaining to Belle about us," Candace said. It was obvious she couldn't stop worrying about it.

"This summer is already a bummer," Jenna said.

"C'mon, guys," Nat urged, "let's hit reset. Let's promise one another that this will be the best summer yet. We've got a great bunk and we can have lots of fun, right?" She raised her hand. "High five!"

"Right!" the gang cried, high-fiving her.

And then a bloodcurdling scream blasted Nat's eardrums.

"What was *that*?" she asked.

A second scream filled the air. It was coming from their cabin.

"C'mon, you guys!" Nat shouted.

She broke into a run, abandoning her half of the duffel. Brynn did the same. Tori set down her suitcase and jetted to catch up.

And everyone raced forwards as a *third* scream erupted from the top of the hill.

"Spider!" Valerie shrieked as she leaped on top of the toilet seat in the 5A bathroom stall. The gold and purple beads on her braids clacked together as she covered her mouth with both hands and knocked her knees together. "Big hairy spider!"

Belle raced into the bathroom with a clipboard containing a thick wad of paperwork pressed against her chest. She was wearing a black spaghetti-strap tank top, black walking shorts and black flip-flops. She had dark circles under her enormous chocolate brown eyes, and her hair flew behind her like a short black cape.

"Where is it?" Belle asked, dashing into the bathroom and scanning the tile floor. "Look out. It might be poisonous."

Chelsea and Gaby raced into the bathroom after Belle, nearly wedging themselves in the doorway as they both tried to enter at the same time.

"What's wrong?" Chelsea shouted.

"Spider!" Valerie jabbed her index finger at the shower stall. Valerie could have sworn the insect had doubled in size since she had first spotted it. It was a mutant! "Eek! There!"

"Oh, for heaven's sake," Gaby snorted. The heavily freckled girl with long dark brown hair rolled her eyes as she came up beside Belle. Chelsea hung back. The counsellor, who was squatting on her haunches next to the shower, was watching Valerie's nemesis as it extended a big, huge, furry leg to examine the tiled lip of the shower stall.

"That little speck?" Gaby bent over to inspect the invader.

"It's a wicked scary speck," Valerie insisted. "It might be a black widow."

"Well, it'll be a dead black widow soon enough." Gaby started to pull off her sandal when Belle waved her away.

"No, Gaby. It's not a black widow. It's just a common house spider. I'll take it outside."

Valerie fully expected Belle to slide the spider onto her clipboard or grab it with a wad of toilet paper, but instead, she held the clipboard against her chest with her forearms and scooped the spider into her left palm with her right hand. She was *touching* the insectoid lifeform! *"Please* take it away," Valerie begged.

Just then, the door slammed open again, and a stampede of footfalls thundered into the bunk.

"What's the matter? What's wrong?" voices called. Valerie recognized the lovely blend of her CLFs – Camp Lakeview Friends – Natalie, Tori, Alex, Alyssa, Jenna, Brynn and Candace. With a joyful yelp, she executed a flawless *grand jeté* off the toilet seat and galloped past Belle, Chelsea and Gaby out of the bathroom.

"Hi!" she cried, dancing into a big group hug that included all of her friends.

"Val, what's the matter?" Natalie demanded, studying Valerie's face, then craning her neck to see into the bathroom. "Who was screaming?"

"Me, girlfriend! There's a humongous big spider."

Valerie motioned to the girls to put a lot of distance between them and the bathroom.

"It was a tiny little spider," Gaby sniped as she and Chelsea came out of the bathroom as well. Gaby shook her head in disgust. Chelsea just looked at the floor.

"Coming through." Belle's flip-flops smacked against the soles of her feet as she swerved around the crowd of girls. Her hands were cupped together as she pushed open the door with her hip and went outside.

"She's carrying the spider. In her bare hands," Valerie whispered.

Brynn's brows shot up. "Wow. Cool. Nature woman."

"Crazy woman," Valerie said. "Yick."

"You are such a baby," Gaby said to Valerie. Then she walked as far from the big pile-up of friends as she could. She turned and looked expectantly at Chelsea, raising a brow and practically giving her sandalled foot an impatient tap-tap-tap. It wasn't everyone who could boss Chelsea around, but Gaby was definitely a world-class bully.

Chelsea stayed where she was for a moment, then walked around the other girls and crossed the cabin to join her. She was still looking at the floor. The two stood between the bunk furthest from the bathroom and the CIT's single bed as if the other girls were radioactive.

"When did you get in?" Alex asked Valerie, as if trying to pick up where she had left off. "We haven't seen you all day."

Valerie stuffed her hands in the pockets of her baggy light green shorts. "My stepmother drove me down the back way," she said, feeling the warm fuzzies. She and Sharin were getting along so well. "I was going to join you in the parking lot, but Belle said you'd probably be back soon."

"She was right," Brynn said. "And we got back a lot sooner because we heard you screaming."

Valerie laughed. "Now I know how to make you hustle."

Brynn smiled too. She looked around the bunk, her smile flickering a little when she got to Chelsea and Gaby.

"We're all here now except for Priya," Brynn noted. "Have you seen her?" She looked from Valerie to Chelsea and Gaby.

Valerie shook her head, while Gaby and Chelsea didn't react at all.

"I just got here and dumped my stuff." Valerie pointed to a large dark purple carryall silk-screened with FUSION SPACE DANCE WORKS in black letters.

"I hope everything's okay," Brynn murmured.

Gaby muttered something to Chelsea that Valerie

couldn't hear. Jenna caught Valerie's attention and gave her head a little shake as if to say, *Don't bother with those two.*

Already? Valerie wondered.

"What about David, Jenna? Have you seen him?" Tori asked.

Jenna shrugged as if she didn't really care if David showed. "I guess he's not here yet."

Valerie figured Jenna was still feeling awkward about the way things had turned out between David and Sarah. David and Sarah had been a couple until the Memorial Day weekend at Jenna's lake house, when David started liking Jenna. And then Sarah didn't come back this summer. Sarah had insisted that she and Abby preferred sports camp to Camp Lakeview, but Valerie knew Jenna was concerned that all the boyfriend–girlfriend stuff had influenced that decision. That made two more of the double-bunk CLFs who weren't here.

Just as Valerie shot Jenna a look of support – they had traded a lot of e-mail on the subject – Belle came back into the cabin. She breezed through the main room and returned to the bathroom. Valerie heard the sound of rushing water, and she assumed Belle was washing her hands.

The fruity tang of moisturizer permeated the air as Belle reappeared, rubbing her hands and forearms.

"Crisis averted. And the spider has been returned to the wild." She didn't smile, and Valerie was embarrassed that she had gone all hyper about the bug. She just had a thing about spiders.

Then Belle studied her clipboard, her lips moving as she read something off it. She was very pale and thin. Valerie wondered if she'd been sick. There was a vibe surrounding her that Valerie couldn't quite figure out. She just wasn't what Valerie had come to expect from a summer camp counsellor. Not bubbly. Not someone to gently tease her about her spider freak-out and reassure all the girls that she had the matter well in hand.

"It looks like we're almost all here." Belle squinted as she counted heads. "One missing." She glanced down at her clipboard. "You three were on the bus, and I've met Valerie, so I'm guessing it's Priya Shah."

"Correct," Alex told her. Since she was such an old hand at camp, she often fell into the role of helping the counsellors – especially new ones. Sometimes she even went to the kitchen after dinner to help Pete and the CITs do the dishes.

Belle made a notation on her clipboard. Then she looked up at the group with a crooked smile.

"I'm Belle Hogan. I'm from Maine and this is my first summer at Camp Lakeview. I was a CIT last year in Bangor."

"So this is your first year as a camp counsellor," Alex said slowly.

"Yes," Belle said. "Apparently I'm the second Belle that Chelsea has known," she added, including Chelsea in the conversation. "She has a friend back home named Belle."

Chelsea shrugged as if that was no big deal. Gaby frowned at Chelsea.

"You never told me that."

"I don't have to tell you everything," Chelsea shot back.

Woo, snotty much? Valerie thought as a dull red spread beneath Gaby's freckles. Valerie hadn't been very happy to discover that both Chelsea *and* Gaby were in her bunk. She figured the others felt that way too. They were both very difficult to deal with – even when they were dealing with each other.

"Where's our CIT?" Natalie asked Belle.

"Clarissa went down to the office to let them know Valerie arrived," Belle said. "You probably just missed each other." She looked at Natalie, Tori and Alyssa. "Let's see." Tilting her head, she paused and pressed her finger to her lips. She looked washed out. Maybe it was all the black clothes.

She pointed at Tori.

"You're our California girl."

"Like, totally," Tori replied in a fake Valley girl accent as she moved her shoulders and hips to her own inner groove thang. The other girls chuckled — except for Gaby and Chelsea, who folded their arms and rolled their eyes.

"Alyssa, the artist," Belle said, gesturing to Alyssa's dramatic butterfly earrings. "Which leaves New York Natalie." She tilted her head as she gave Natalie a once-over.

"Guilty," Natalie said with a grin.

"Well, I know that you've all bunked together before," Belle said, "so we'll dispense with my get-to-know-you game."

"Is that the one where we get a bunch of candy to share?" Jenna asked hopefully. "Because you know, we do need to catch up." Jenna ate candy and sweets practically 24/7. She was such a jock that she burned up all the calories. Even though Valerie took dance, she couldn't hope to eat as much as Jenna Bloom and still fit into her leotard and tights.

"We do not need to catch up," Brynn insisted. "We e-mail one another practically every day."

"*Some* of us," Chelsea said quietly. Then she added quickly, "I want a top bunk."

"Me too," Gaby said. "This bunk." She put her hand on the bunk beside the counsellor and CIT's annex.

Then she jerked it away as if she had processed that spending an entire summer one bed over from their counsellors was maybe not the best move – plus it was also the bunk furthest away from the bathroom. She extended her arm towards the bunk behind Valerie.

"Wait. I want *that* bunk."

"Remember, we're not going to pick bunks until everyone has arrived," Belle said.

"Well, Priya's late," Gaby argued. "We're all supposed to arrive before the cookout. The rest of us are here, and the cookout's going to start in a few minutes."

"We'll wait for Priya before we pick out our bunks," Belle repeated, and there was that edge to her voice again. "So you'll have to wait until after the cookout to unpack and put your things away in your cubbies."

"Speaking of which, we left our stuff on the path," Natalie said. "We'll have to go get everything quickly before the raccoons snag it. Nature can be so cruel."

"That's a joke, right?" Tori asked worriedly. "I mean, they won't really start pawing through my stuff, right?"

"Not unless they can get your suitcase unzipped." Natalie grinned at her stricken expression. "I'm just teasing."

"Then after we get the cabin organized tonight," Belle continued, "I think a moonlight hike is in order."

"Aren't those silent?" Valerie said, sounding less than thrilled.

"We can eat, though," Jenna volunteered. "My mom sent some cupcakes."

"Oh, I've been dreaming about those cupcakes!" Valerie cried. "They are to die for!"

"'To die for.' Touch wood." Tori rapped her fingers on the bunk's wooden wall.

"Sounds good." Belle returned her attention to her clipboard.

"About the hike," Tori went on. "And, well, dying. Um, are you sure it's safe to walk around in the dark?"

Belle cocked an eyebrow without lifting her eyes from the clipboard. She made a check mark about halfway down the page. "Of course I'm sure. We'll stay on the paths and stick together. Why wouldn't it be safe?"

"Did they tell you about Cropsy?" Tori took a deep breath. "About the anniversary?"

"'They'?" Belle finally looked up at her.

"Dr. Steve," Tori said. "He didn't say *anything* about Cropsy?"

"No." Belle tapped the back of her clipboard with her pen. "But maybe you should."

"He's this psycho-guy," Tori began. "He stalks campers. And every six years—"

There was whooping and crazed laughter outside. A whole lot of it.

"That's my brother's voice," Jenna said suspiciously.

She went outside. "Adam!" she bellowed. "You huge dork! Put that down!"

She ducked her head back into the room. "Tori, they got into your suitcase! Adam has on your bikini top!"

"He *what*?" Tori shouted.

Jenna, Tori, Natalie, Alyssa and Brynn burst out of the cabin.

"Adam, you geek, give that back or I'll strangle you with it!" Jenna yelled, and the other girls started shrieking and whooping.

Maybe this will be a normal summer after all, Valerie thought, grinning to herself.

CHAPTER THREE

Inside the cabin, Belle laid her clipboard against her chest again and walked to the bunk's door. She looked out, watching, then she went outside.

"Boys, enough! Give those things back to the girls. *Now.*"

Her voice trailed off. Valerie assumed she was going down the hill to the scene of the crime.

The whooping faded. Valerie's friends stopped screaming.

After a few more seconds, Belle came back into the cabin, shaking her head with a sigh. "Crisis averted," she announced.

Go, Belle, Valerie thought admiringly.

Belle tapped her finger against the paper on her clipboard.

"Next on the list. Please give me your cellphones and electronics. BlackBerrys, iPods, Game Boys and whatever else has been invented in the last five minutes."

Valerie reluctantly parted with her cellphone and her iPod. The other girls started going through their bags and daypacks, pulling out their cellphones.

"Now we're cut off from civilization," Candace said in a stricken tone as she handed her phone to Belle.

"Oh, right. Cut off except for the phones and computers in the administration building," Gaby snapped. "I don't know why you guys even bothered bringing your cellphones. *I* left mine at home."

"We'll still be able to e-mail our parents on Sundays, right?" Chelsea asked as she carried her cellphone to Belle's bed. Valerie caught the anxious note in her voice.

"Yes, same as always," Belle assured her. "Dr. Steve has a list outside his office where you can sign up for specific slots to send your e-mail from the office desktop."

Then a high-pitched siren blared through the cabin, and everybody jumped. It whined and keened like a wounded water buffalo. And Valerie actually knew what a wounded water buffalo sounded like from her African unit in geography.

"From your reactions, I'd guess that the siren is new," Belle said. "That means it's time for the cookout. You guys can go on down when you're ready."

47

"Good," Gaby said coldly. "I'm ready. Come on, Chelsea."

She didn't even look at the other girls as she and Chelsea left the bunk. Tapping her clipboard with her pen, Belle watched them go.

Jenna, Alyssa, Tori, Brynn and Natalie stumbled back into the bunk carrying a big duffel bag and a black suitcase. A stretchy purple bikini top dangled from Tori's fist.

Jenna shook her head in total disgust. "My brother and his friends are so immature."

"At least we got everything back," Tori said.

"Yeah, in return for a bribe. *Three* precious cupcakes," Jenna groused. "He got his own stash from my mom. He's such a pig."

"I need your cellphones and iPods," Belle told them.

The girls complied. Then the bunkmates filed into the bathroom by twos and threes to spritz off and check themselves out in the mirror above the two white porcelain sinks. Valerie watched as nearly all the girls glammed it up a notch and redid their hair. Tori and Natalie brought out the big guns – colourful plastic pouches brimming with make-up and make-up brushes. Alex just combed her short, straight black hair, while Valerie applied the bronze-tint eyeshadow that Sharin had given her for her birthday.

As Alex put her comb away, she smiled at Valerie's reflection in the mirror. "It's so good to see you." Then she laughed and added, "Even though I just saw you a month ago."

"Same here," Valerie said warmly.

Jenna popped in. "Can you tell I streaked my hair?" She moved her head left and right. Golden tendrils gleamed among her light brown curls.

"Yes. Very sassy," Valerie said.

"Thanks. Hey, do you think Chelsea highlighted her hair?" Jenna asked, examining a strand in the mirror. "It looked blonder to me. But I could be remembering it wrong. She didn't send any pictures."

"I don't think she went on our double-bunk blog at all," Alex said. "Do you remember reading anything from her?"

"No." Valerie daubed some bronzer on her cheekbones. "She didn't post. Neither did Gaby."

"I think Chelsea's hair is the same as last year," Alex said.

"So is her attitude," Jenna grumped. "I really will try to get along with her," she added, before either of them could say anything. "And Gaby." She sighed and glanced towards the main room, where Belle was sitting. "But is it okay to privately wish they weren't in our bunk?"

"Privately," Alex murmured. She wrinkled her nose. "And, privately? I wish the same thing."

"Me too," Valerie added. "Privately."

When Valerie came out of the bathroom, Belle was sitting cross-legged on her bed, hunched over her clipboard as she wrote furiously. Valerie hoped she hadn't heard Alex, Jenna and her talking about Gaby and Chelsea.

Out of simple curiosity, she tilted her head, trying to see what Belle was doing, but Belle jerked and glanced up sharply at her.

"Yes?" she said, sounding a little brusque as she flipped the clipboard over and pressed her palms down on it.

"Oh, sorry." Valerie started to move away.

"It's all right. You just startled me, Valerie." She kept her hands on the clipboard. "Is there something you wanted?" Her voice still sounded edgy. Was her left eye actually twitching?

"No. I'm good," Valerie replied, still feeling awkward. First she'd freaked Belle out with the spider incident, and now she had accidentally snooped into Belle's private counsellor business. She wasn't starting out very well with her new counsellor.

Semi-dejected, she went outside. Jenna followed after her, moving away from the door and looking over her shoulder.

"What was *that* all about?" Jenna whispered.

Valerie shook her head. "She didn't want me to see what she was writing down, I guess. Maybe it was something confidential."

"Yeah, but she didn't have to strangle her clipboard to keep it from talking." Jenna pantomimed choking herself. "Belle...killed...the...clipboard. It knew too much!"

Valerie laughed. Belle's reaction *had* been pretty extreme.

Natalie joined them. In addition to a lot of make-up, she had put on some perfume. She looked as if she had stepped out of the pages of *Teen Vogue* to go to a prom, and not to a camp cookout. "Who killed what?"

Valerie described what had happened as Brynn joined the party. She kept her voice low and moved the group away from the door. She didn't want Belle to overhear them.

"Maybe Belle was writing up some kind of incident report," Brynn said. "About what we said about being stuck with Gaby and Chelsea." She had on perfume, too. Valerie wondered if it was the same perfume Jordan had bought Brynn for her birthday. What was it like to get a present like that from a guy?

51

"Maybe she's reporting us," Candace fretted.

Alex looked troubled. "I always like my counsellors a lot. But Belle..." She made a little face. "I don't know. Maybe I just have low blood sugar."

"Then let's eat!" Jenna cried, jog-walking down the steep hill past them.

"Careful," Alex called after her. "It's awfully early in the summer to go to the ER." After stepping into a groundhog hole last summer, Jenna had wound up in a cast, and she had had to sit out most of the events in Colour War. Luckily, there had been a pie-eating contest and Jenna, with her love of sweets, had won the event for the Reds.

"Hey, girls!" Clarissa shouted as she trudged up the hill towards them. Her eyes rested on Val for an extra second. "Hey, you," she added. "I was wondering when I'd finally get to see you today." She leaned in and gave Val a hug. Then she continued towards their cabin. "I need to go talk to Belle, but I'll see you all at dinner, okay?" She walked a few more steps before turning around to add in one more thought. "I'm so glad I'm working with your bunk."

The five girls exchanged devilish grins. "So are we!" Val shouted back.

"So. Are. We," she said more quietly to her friends.

They continued tramping down the hill. The vast

lake glistened in the distance. The shadows had lengthened, and overhead, thunderclouds rumbled. Valerie wondered if they would be able to go on the hike tonight.

Everything seems kind of off, she thought as she gazed around at her friends. *Maybe I should have gone to dance camp in Philly, like LaToya.* But that would have meant spending the summer *with* LaToya, and frankly, Valerie needed a break from her imperious stepsister.

The thing was, though, she was starting to wonder if she needed a break from Camp Lakeview, too.

I thought we would have good times with a fun counsellor like last year, Valerie thought. *But so far, it looks like it's us versus Gaby and Chelsea, and I've managed to tick off Belle. What is in those pages that she doesn't want me to see? She doesn't seem like the camp counsellor type at all.*

Maybe it's just me. Maybe I'm not the camper type any more. I don't feel right here. Something's wrong. The others are noticing it too.

An owl hooted. It was the middle of the day, when owls should be asleep, right? Valerie wasn't sure. She was a city girl. She didn't know much about birds and raccoons and nature stuff.

Then something moved inside the branches of a pine tree as she passed it, and she jerked.

For heaven's sake, she thought, *I'm acting like such a baby.*

But she couldn't shake the feeling that she had better stay on her guard.

On the other side of Shadow Lake, Jeremiah Wheatly lowered his binoculars and smiled.

"She's here."

His friend Dan nodded absently as he bent over the hull of the overturned dinghy. A wide crack ran down the centre.

"Good. Stop spying on her and hand me the chainsaw."

Jeremiah bent down and picked up the bulky object with his one good hand. It was hard to learn how to do things with one arm. His whole life had changed since the accident.

Dan grabbed the starter cord, tugged hard, and let the chainsaw rip.

"Careful with that thing. You wouldn't want to cut off your arm," Jeremiah said over the roar of the engine.

They both laughed.

"I have to do something to get her to notice me this year," Jeremiah half-shouted.

"Well, what's she into?"

Jeremiah thought a moment. "She likes ice cream."

"Then give her some ice cream."

"She also said she likes horror movies and roller coasters and Stephen King novels."

"Sounds like she likes a good scare," Dan offered. "It's perfect. Give her some ice cream and then just scare her right into your arms!"

"Sounds like a plan," Jeremiah yelled.

The chainsaw whined.

Last to leave the bunk, Belle picked up the box of electronic items and headed for the screen door. Just as she began to push it open, her own cellphone trilled inside her daypack. She shifted the box to her hip, unzipped the pack, and hurriedly fished out the phone.

"Hello?" She nodded, listening. "So far, so good. I'm keeping an eye on them."

She listened hard. Then she took a deep breath. "Yes, I understand. Let's just hope it doesn't come to that." She shut the phone and replaced it in her pack.

Then she went out the door to join her unsuspecting campers.

CHAPTER FOUR

Jenna inhaled the yummalicious aroma of hamburgers on the grill as 5A reached the grassy expanse beside the lake. The yellow diving dock shone in the sun. She had conquered her fear of diving two summers ago. What would she master this year?

Pete, Dr. Steve and Susan, the head counsellor of the fourth division, were manning the oversize grill. All three gave Jenna a friendly wave as she grabbed a paper plate and joined the line of campers waiting for food. Brynn and the rest of their group came up behind her – Tori after Brynn, then Natalie, Valerie, Candace, Alex and Alyssa. There was no sign of Gaby or Chelsea.

Then...there he was. David.

He was standing with a bunch of guys by the big wooden pagoda, laughing and eating a hot dog. He had freckles across his nose, just like her. And thick lashes around his light green eyes. And a super-sweet smile.

What total girlbait.

He didn't see her, and she ducked her head, suddenly very shy. She hadn't seen him since Memorial Day weekend at her family's lake house. They had e-mailed a lot and spoken on the phone a few times, but to see him here, in person...she swallowed hard. He had gone from liking Sarah to liking her. Maybe he would decide to like someone else here at camp. Jenna was new to the whole "like" thing. She didn't know how to spot the signs if the guy you were totally into decided to move on. Besides, she wasn't even sure if she *was* totally into David.

Well, okay, that wasn't true. Her heart was pounding and her hands were sweaty. From taking two summers' worth of the zillions of surveys and quizzes that Natalie read aloud from her fashion magazines, Jenna knew those were two of the signs of true like.

"Jen!" he cried as he looked up and spotted her.

"Oh, there he is," Brynn murmured, as if she were crushing on David too. Jenna felt a prickle of confusion and jealousy, until she ticked her glance to the left. Jordan, Priya and Spence were headed for them as well. She realized that Brynn had been talking about Jordan, not David. And, ooh, interesting note: Priya was walking with Spence. During the school year, Priya had had a crush on a guy named Riley. But that had fizzled out. Everyone knew Spence had liked Priya since the

Washington DC field trip last summer. Was Priya now into him, too?

"Hey," David said, reaching Jenna's side.

She was stunned. He had grown at least half a metre! Okay, maybe ten centimetres. Okay, maybe two centimetres. A whole two centimetres since May!

"Hi," she said. "Fancy meeting you here."

He cracked up like she had said the funniest thing he had ever heard. Her eyes grew a little wider. There were bits of stubble on his cheeks and under his nose. David was shaving!

"Heya, Brynners," Jordan said as he walked up to the line, giving Brynn a quick, shy hug as Priya squealed happily and bear-hugged Jenna, then Brynn, then went on down the row of girls.

"Guess what, you guys!" Priya said. "We got lost on the way to camp!"

"No way." Brynn's forehead wrinkled. "Is everything okay?"

"Duh," Priya teased her. "We're here, aren't we?"

"We *did* almost run out of gas," Jordan said. "I was just about to strap the ol' gas can on Priya and send her foraging for supplies out in the forest. But when she got out of the car, she saw the Camp Lakeview sign." He shook his head. "Which is not very helpful when it's lying in a ditch."

"In a ditch?" Tori asked. "Which way did you come?"

"The same way as the bus," Priya said. "It was by total accident that we saw the sign." She blushed. "We had to pull over because I was feeling a little carsick. Just one kilometre from camp, I decided I needed some fresh air."

"However, she did not barf, I am happy to report," Jordan added, nudging her. Then he ducked and added, "But she could blow any second! And believe me when I tell you that Priya hurling is most impressive!"

"*Jordan*," Priya said between clenched teeth. It was obvious to Jenna that she was mortified to be discussing the subject in front of Spence.

"One kilometre?" Tori persisted. "The Camp Lakeview sign said one kilometre? And it was in a ditch?"

"Yeah." Priya and Jordan both nodded. "And heavily spray-painted."

Natalie, Tori and Alyssa looked puzzled. "What's wrong?" Jordan asked.

"When we passed that sign, it was upright. And it wasn't spray-painted," Tori said.

"Maybe it was a different sign," Jordan ventured. "But ours was in a ditch and it had been spray-painted with the words, 'Go back.'"

"In big red capital letters," Priya added.

"Red like blood?" Tori asked anxiously.

"Red like primer, more likely." Jordan gazed at the girls. "Hey, you're all freaked out. No big, chicks. It was obviously a prank."

"Right," Tori said slowly. Then she said, "Was the paint wet?"

"I didn't check," Priya said. "I wanted to get here." She frowned. "But Jordan's right. It's no big deal."

"No, it *is* a big deal," Tori said again. "It's Cropsy. I know it is!"

"What's a Cropsy?" Priya asked.

"A homicidal maniac who lives in the woods," Tori began.

Jordan started snickering. "No way."

"Yes," Tori argued. "It's a true story. Every six years, he..." She scrunched up her face as Jordan snickered some more.

"He what?" Priya urged Tori, nodding at her.

"I'll tell you later," Tori said, giving Jordan a pretend evil eye, but in a friendly way. "When certain people aren't around."

"'Certain people'?" Jordan asked, pressing his fingertips against his chest. "Me?"

Tori nodded. "Yes."

Jordan made his hands into claws and pawed the air.

"By then, it may be too late, mwahaha."

"It's too late for you, anyway," Tori said. "I'm pretty sure you're on his list."

"The list of death?" Jordan shot back. He grabbed his neck and made his mossy green eyes bulge out. "Tooooo...laaate for meeee. Run, Brynn. Run, Priiiiyaaaa."

"You shouldn't tease," Tori said. "Or you really *will* be on his list."

From her place in line ahead of them, Valerie snapped her fingers.

"*That's* what our counsellor was doing! She was making the list of Cropsy's new victims. I thought I heard her muttering 'Jordan' while she was writing."

Priya smiled evilly at Jordan. "Right. Cropsy. She keeps track of all the people who dare to make fun of him."

"Then I'm dead," Jordan said, rolling his eyes in theatrical sorrow.

"I am going to miss you," Priya said. "All those years of beating you at Horse. Of inventing disgusting concoctions for you to eat when I whup you at wall-ball. Of watching your 'Spoon' spoon slide down your ski-slope nose. How very sad." She sighed.

Jordan sighed along with her. "Brynn, will *you* miss me?"

Amused, Brynn hugged her empty plate against her chest. "I'll bring flowers to your grave every opening day of camp," she promised. "Unless, of course, I'm *at* camp." She pantomimed tossing the plate over her shoulder.

"Maybe I could get buried here, then," Jordan suggested helpfully.

"I have a very serious question," David asked. Then he started laughing. "If Jordan dies during the cookout, can I have his hamburger?"

"Humph. I don't think I *will* die any time this summer, if that's the way you guys are going to be," Jordan huffed. "Dead and disrespected. Not going there."

"Who says the choice is up to you?" Tori asked softly.

She turned to Jenna. "Bloom, you've been coming here the longest of anyone," she said. "Have you heard about Cropsy?"

"Kinda sorta," Jenna said, wrinkling her forehead. All the Bloom kids had gone to Lakeview for years and years. Stephanie had even been a counsellor. "I vaguely remember Steph talking about him a few years ago. But I think she thought he was just a camp legend."

Jenna wondered if Adam remembered anything about Cropsy.

"He's not a legend," Tori said. "He's a real person."

"Cropsy's not the real threat. The lions are really the ones to watch out for," Jordan declared. At their questioning looks, he spread his arms wide.

"You haven't heard about the man-eating lions of Shadow Lake?"

He dropped his voice. "Long ago, there was a circus train that came through this very part of Pennsylvania. The train crashed. The lions got free and ran off into the woods. They gobbled up all the rabbits, and then they gobbled up all the squirrels, and then they started gobbling up the local kids."

"What a relief," Priya drawled. "Just the *local* kids. Like that ice-cream guy who always gives us extra scoops."

"Jeremiah," Jenna said. She grinned. "I think he was crushing on Clarissa last year."

"Ooh, we'll have to check that out when we go into town," Brynn enthused. "Let's ask Belle if we can do a town run on Sunday." Sundays were special days for fifth division campers – they had a late brunch and then they got to laze around and do stuff like go into town for treats and shopping. Not that there was much to buy except little patchwork teddy bears and a cookbook put out by the volunteer fire department auxiliary and knick-knacks like that.

"Please, ladies, this is not about crushes," Jordan reminded them. "After they ate all the locals, they started gobbling up Lakeview campers. Remember Tom Esposito?"

"He had to go home last summer because he had glandular fever," Priya said.

"That's just what they told us." Jordan pursed his lips and growled. *"Rrroarrrrr."*

"Really?" Candace asked in a strangled voice. Her lids flickered as if she might faint.

"Really," Jordan said, his mouth twitching.

"He's making it up," Priya told her. "He's such a kidder." She smacked Jordan on the arm. "Don't freak out my bunkbud with your hideous lies, Jordan."

"Ow!" He rubbed his bicep and caught Priya's wrist as she prepared to punch him again. "Okay, okay, it's all a hideous lie," he told Candace. "Or, as we say, a tall tale," he said to Priya. "Urban legend. No harm meant."

"Okay," Candace murmured. "Good."

Everyone got their hot dogs, burgers and sides, and found places beside the lake to sit and eat. David stuck close to Jenna, which made for much happiness. Even nicer, her idiot twin Adam stayed way far away.

No doubt he was still waiting for the three cupcakes she owed him.

Jordan didn't hang with Brynn as much as Jenna had expected he would. Mostly he chatted with all the 5A girls, and he kept getting up and leaving to say hi to guys he knew. By the pensive look on Brynn's face, Jenna could see that she was disappointed.

Why did we ever start liking boys? she wondered. *They are so confusing.*

Then David said, "I'm going to go get another hamburger. Would you like one, Jenna?" and Jenna went all warm and gushy. How thoughtful!

"No, thanks," she said, trying to keep the telltale sounds of total luuurve out of her reply.

"I'll go with you, man." Spence jumped up, rubbing some twigs and leaves off the butt of his cargo shorts.

The two trotted off. Jenna slid a glance over at Priya, who was looking a little goony as she watched Spence go.

"Ca-*yute*," Jenna drawled.

Priya giggled. "It's weird to start liking a guy I used to argue with about whose farts lit better."

"It's weird to start liking guys, period," Jenna replied.

"This is true." Priya took a bite of potato salad.

"Very true." Jenna sipped her bug juice.

David came back a few minutes later with his hamburger, but no Spence. Jenna looked at David questioningly, but he gave her a frown and shook his head, clueless about what she was asking him. So as nonchalantly as she could, she turned her head and gazed at the food line, then at the kids gathered by the redwood picnic tables, sitting on the ground under the pine trees and on the large boulders.

She found Spence.

He was leaning forward with one leg propped on a boulder, his plate empty, his face lit up like he had just found out that he had won the lottery. And he was talking to a girl. But not just any girl.

He was talking to Chelsea!

Chelsea sat on the boulder with her plate balanced on her knees. Spence said something and she covered her mouth with her fingertips, threw back her head, and laughed.

Stunned to the roots of her highlights, Jenna drew in her breath and turned back around. Priya had no idea that potential disaster had struck. She had not seen Spence with Snark Girl. Innocent and unsuspecting, she was still eating her potato salad.

Jenna had to process this. Spence: a guy who was officially in like with Priya, or at least, had been last summer, flirting with Chelsea.

Back to the guys-are-weird equation, she thought. *Oh, yeah.*

"Are you okay?" David asked, peering at her.

Priya looked at her too. Red alert, red alert. Jenna had to come up with a distraction right here and now. She did *not* want Priya to see Spence flirting with Chelsea. Surely the boy would come to his senses in the next thirty seconds and get his twig-free butt back over here.

"Oh, well, you know, it's a little awkward, um, about you and me," she said to David, covering her shock with the first thing that came to her mind. Which was *not* the best thing. *Yikes! Delete that convo, Bloom!*

"What?" he asked, blinking his gorgeous but clueless eyes.

Why did I start this? "Well." She took a breath. "You know, Sarah and all."

He blinked at her again. "What about Sarah?"

Priya went back to eating her potato salad, as if to give them privacy.

"Because...you and she..." She trailed off, suddenly discovering how fascinating the grass was.

"Sarah and I broke up," he said simply, "because I like you. And she was fine with that."

"Um. Right." The grass was green. Very green.

David peered at her. "And? Aren't *you* fine with it?"

67

"Um, well, I just want to make sure the *other* girls are okay with it." Green and a little slippery, actually.

"The other girls?" She could hear his bewilderment. "What does that matter...why...?"

Pasting a smile on her face, she gave her hand a wave as if to erase the entire humiliating discussion. Which she desperately wanted to do. Little bits of grass fluttered to the ground like flat green snowflakes.

"Never mind," she said. "It's girl logic."

"Okay." He shrugged. By his blank, untroubled expression, it was obvious that he was not only okay with it, but that he had already moved on past it. "So," he said. "Did you know that your brother can stuff six hot dogs into his mouth at the same time?"

Priya guffawed.

Beside the lake, the shadows lengthened and the campers started trickling away, heading for their bunks to work on their electives and digest way too many cookout delicacies. Chelsea discovered that Gaby had snagged the last hot dog on the grill even though Chelsea had called dibs on it. After she denounced Gaby's wretched thievery, she started pouting.

Priya heaved a quiet sigh. No one, absolutely no one, could pout like Chelsea.

But in this case, Chelsea's pouting was a good thing. Because as soon as she thrust out her lower lip, Spence drifted back to Priya. Priya's stomach did a little flip when he asked if he could sit on the grass next to her, and then it tied itself in a knot. He had spent a long time talking to Chelsea. A *long* time. What the heck was up with that?

He can't like her, can he? If we don't like her, then how can he?

But of course she couldn't ask him about it. She couldn't ask him if she had been imagining things or if he had gone blind or insane. One of the rules of girls liking boys was that you did *not* discuss your competition. If you had competition, you pretended you didn't know about it.

But Priya knew. Boy, did she know. And if she hadn't known, Chelsea's smug grin would have informed her, thank you very much. *Not.*

Spence left to go with his bunk – 5B – and Priya's bunk climbed back up the hill to the cabin. Priya's stomach was full of way too much potato salad; her mind was full of questions; and she got more and more nervous trudging up the hill. If Chelsea started talking about Spence like they had a thing, Priya really would hurl.

The tall pines threw shadows across the path and Priya stood for a moment in the relative coolness of the shade. She tilted back her chin and closed her eyes. Her forehead was sweaty and she wished she didn't feel so sick.

She got the distinct feeling that someone was watching her, and she hoped it was Spence, seeking her forgiveness for his complete insanity and lack of taste. But when she opened her eyes, there was no one there.

I could have sworn...

Priya shrugged and headed back up to the cabin.

Once everyone had returned, Belle assigned chores and everyone picked bunks. Chelsea and Gaby both wanted the same top bunk, and they spent so much time arguing over it that all the other top bunks got called. So Belle solved their dilemma by tossing a coin, and Chelsea won. Now it was Gaby's turn to pout. She was very impressive. Maybe Spence would start liking Gaby now, too.

Next, Clarissa began the process of assigning everyone their electives. Priya was one of the first to go and she got both her choices, nature and newspaper. Given how hot the weather was, she was glad she hadn't asked for sports. One by one the others met with the CIT, and Gaby got what *she* wanted – arts and crafts and nature – while Chelsea wound up in drama and photography, neither of which was her first choice.

Priya couldn't help her pathetic joy at seeing Chelsea's disappointment.

As a result, Chelsea kicked up her pouting a notch. No one said anything, but maybe it was the presence of two world-class pouters in the same bunk that had an effect on everyone else. Priya could feel the tension in the dying sunlight, and as she finished unpacking and putting her clothes away in her cubby, she saw a lot of frowns and heard a lot of sighs.

After that, they went down for dinner, and Priya thought that many of the other campers in the mess hall seemed as grumpy and short-tempered as 5A. Usually the first dinner was a riot of high spirits, laughter, and bunk cheers created on the spot. Bunks tried to goof one another – putting salt in the bug juice, planting plastic spiders in the meat loaf, and sure, there was some of that.

But it wasn't the usual wacky high jinks. Instead, people picked at their meals, complaining that it was too hot to eat heavy food like meat loaf, mashed potatoes and gravy, especially after the cookout.

During dessert – room temperature canned fruit cocktail – Dr. Steve, the tall camp director with thinning blond hair, rattled off a ton of announcements, very few of which interested Priya; then he concluded by declaring that the traditional campwide play would be *The Legend of Sleepy Hollow*. Some of the campers woo-hooed and pumped their arms, but Priya thought it was a strange choice. The story of the Headless Horseman might be too scary for the little kids, especially the new campers who were away from home for the first time.

"I'm trying out for Katrina," Tori announced. "She's Dutch. I've got the look!" She gave her blonde hair a toss.

"Maybe I'll try out too," Natalie said. "Katrina can be a dark-haired Dutch girl."

"I'm going to audition, too," Gaby said, scowling. "I'll give the Hollywood brats a run for their money."

Beneath her Malibu tan, Tori paled a little at the dis, but Natalie took Gaby's cut in her stride. "There can be three Katrinas," she said. "We can be the Flying Katrinas!"

"Whatever," Gaby muttered, scooping up fruit cocktail.

"Brynn will get it if she auditions," Chelsea said. "She always gets the good parts."

"Nuh-uh," Brynn said, looking flattered. "After all, Grace got Wendy."

"That was a fluke," Gaby said. "Besides, she won't be here in time to audition because she flunked another class."

Priya winced. She didn't know how Gaby had found that out, but Grace had asked her friends not to share the fact that she'd failed English. As far as bunkwide chatter was concerned, that was to be kept on the down-low.

"Well, I'm sure Grace will get that class aced and be up here in time to help with the play," Priya said.

"Won't *that* be nice," Gaby said, rolling her eyes.

Dinner finally ended. Darkness crept across Camp Lakeview as 5A lugged themselves back up the hill. Thunder rumbled in the distance, and the air lay thick and heavy. Priya wondered if Belle would cancel their hike.

But no. Within minutes, everyone gathered outside the bunk beneath the full moon. Priya's spirits rose a tad. She loved hiking at night. It was a very camplike thing to do.

"Now don't forget. Everyone needs to remain silent as we walk, so we can hear what's out there," Belle said. "It'll take some time for your eyes to adjust to the darkness, but after a little while you'll be able to see. Just in case..." She flicked on an enormous black flashlight. The beam cast a wide angle of light as bright as day.

They started hiking. The pines rose into a blurry sky

73

— no stars, no moon, just clouds. An owl hooted. No one spoke. The only sounds were their footfalls and the occasional hooting of an owl. Jenna edged up to Priya and Priya nodded at her.

"Spence likes you, Priya," Jenna said in a low voice. "You know he does."

Priya managed a weak smile. "You saw, huh? It wasn't just my imagination?"

"I saw him talking to her. That's all I saw. And I saw him leave her and come sit with you."

"Yeah, but she was lording it over me with that smug grin on the way back to the cabin," Priya pointed out.

"She'd lord it over you if she got the last cherry half in the fruit cocktail," Jenna insisted. "Even though she's on record as hating them."

Priya smiled gratefully at her friend. She was beyond thankful for the back-up.

Maybe this summer's going to be all right after all, she thought.

Across the lake, Jeremiah tipped his binoculars towards his eyes. It was hard to do with just one arm. "I wonder what she's doing."

"You've got it bad," Dan said, grinning at his friend.

"I just hope she does too." Jeremiah lowered the

binoculars and gazed in frustration at his friend's dinghy. There was a thick crack along the running board.

"I don't think we're going to get it fixed tonight. We'd probably be wasting our time, anyway." He gazed at Shadow Lake as the fog wafted over the surface. "The lake's quiet."

"Too quiet," Dan said.

"Hey, Tori," Priya whispered as Belle led the bunk into a gulley. Her sneaker came down across a dry twig with a snap, and Tori jumped. "Are you okay?"

"I keep having a funny feeling," Tori whispered back, "like someone's watching us."

"Well, Clarissa's behind us," Priya pointed out. "And Jenna's over there, and—"

"No, not like that," Tori interrupted her. "Like... Cropsy."

"You *need* to tell me that story," Priya said, a hint of excitement shading her words. "Or maybe not, if it's freaking you out so badly. Did Jenna check in with Adam to see what he remembered?"

"I don't know," Tori said. "She didn't mention it and I forgot to ask her."

"Girls, please," Belle remonstrated as she walked ahead of them. "This is a silent hike."

75

"Sorry," Priya whispered. She gave Tori's arm a little squeeze. *"It's okay,"* she mouthed, but she wasn't sure that Tori could see her face.

In the distance, thunder rumbled.

"We should go back," Tori murmured.

"It's okay," Priya said, out loud this time.

"Because it's going to rain," Tori went on.

As if on cue, a platinum flash of lightning zigzagged overhead. The sky broke open, and rain poured down.

The girls shrieked wildly, covering their heads and darting towards overhanging pine boughs, crashing into one another and stumbling in the dark.

Flicking on her powerful flashlight, Belle waved it above her head.

"Stay calm! It's just rain. Let's *walk* back to the cabin."

But people were already charging back the way they had come. Tori zoomed on ahead, but Priya slipped on a rock and minced forward very carefully.

"Go slowly!" Belle insisted. "Walk in my flashlight beam." She aimed her flashlight at the splattered ground.

"Hey, Priya," Alyssa said, catching up to her. "I brought my rainproof jacket. Let's share." She hoisted the jacket over their heads. The rain was coming down so hard that the jacket didn't do much good, and soon

Alyssa and Priya were slip-sliding in mud.

"Easy does it," Belle called after them. "Go slowly, girls. Take your shoes off before you enter the bunk."

They really weren't very far from the cabin, and soon Alyssa and Priya were stamping their muddy shoes on the porch with about five or six other girls. Alyssa held the jacket over Priya while she unlaced her sneakers.

"I am soaked," Alyssa announced.

"Tell me about it." Priya grimaced and yanked one sneaker off. Her wet sock clung to her foot.

Then Priya heard shouting inside the cabin.

"Whoa," Alyssa said. "What is *that*?"

Priya yanked her other sneaker off. Alyssa did the same. Natalie held the door open as she crossed the threshold first, and Priya and Alyssa tumbled in after.

"You tripped me!" Gaby yelled at Chelsea. She was coated from head to toe in dark brown mud, her eyes wide and furious in a mask of coffee-coloured goo.

"I did not," Chelsea insisted, her mouth working to stay relaxed. Then she burst into giggles. Waving her hand in front of her face, she turned her back, struggling to stifle her laughter.

Gaby *did* look pretty funny. Priya screwed up her face, trying not to laugh; then Alyssa, who was also straining to keep a straight face, caught her eye and they both burst into guffaws.

"Oh, you think it's funny?" Gaby yelled, whirling on them.

Natalie joined in, then Brynn. The cabin was filled with laughter.

"You people are *evil*!" Gaby shrieked. She stomped around the cabin, leaving a trail of muddy footprints and splatters of mud on the floor. "Stop laughing at me!"

"It's just mud, Gaby." Jenna combed her fingers through her sopping wet hair. "Lighten up."

"Mind your own business, Jenna Bloom!" Gaby shouted.

"Hey! This bunk *is* my business." Jenna dropped her hands to her sides. "And I have to live with you for two months! So stop all the 'tude and start acting like a human being or..."

"Or what?" Gaby asked, crossing her arms and raising her chin.

Then, as Priya watched in astonishment, Jenna marched over to her bed, which was a lower bunk, where she had laid out some midnight candy "supplies". She picked up a handful of Skittles and threw them at Gaby. One of them hit Gaby's shoulder, but the rest rat-a-tatted onto the floor.

"Or...that!" Jenna cried, and she looked just as surprised as Gaby that she had done it.

"You brat!" Gaby bellowed.

"You're the brat, Gaby!" Priya shouted without thinking. She was shocked. It just came out.

Something *blew* after that. Girls started shouting and yelling, and someone threw a pillow, and Gaby walked right up to Jenna and wiped mud all over the shoulder of her white T-shirt —

— and the door slammed open, hard.

"What is going *on* in here?" Belle thundered. Her black hair was plastered against her head, and her white face looked like a skull. She had her flashlight in her hand.

Everyone was quiet for a moment. Then Gaby pointed a trembling finger at Jenna.

"She started it."

"Look what she did to my T-shirt!" Jenna's voice shook as she gestured to the mud on her shirt. "This won't come out!"

The whole bunk talked at once again.

Belle reached over to the light switch and flicked off the lights. It worked; as 5A was plunged into darkness, all conversation ceased. Priya heard another roll of thunder, and the tapping of the rain on the roof.

Beside Priya, Candace sniffled. "I want to go home," she said.

Me too, Priya thought.

Belle said in a very soft voice, "That's better. Now, I'm turning the light back on. And then we're cleaning this place up, and then we're going to talk."

After everyone showered and hung up their wet clothes, and Chelsea, who had floor duty, cleaned up the mud, Belle ordered them to sit in a circle on the floor. Walking around the perimeter with her arms folded over her chest, she informed them that they had better shape up.

At Belle's prompting, Chelsea apologized to Gaby for laughing at her, but *not* for tripping her, insisting that she hadn't done it and it would be a lie to say she had. Gaby almost started yelling all over again, but Belle told her to settle down.

The others also apologized to Gaby for laughing, and Jenna apologized to Gaby for throwing candy at her. Gaby told Jenna that if the mud didn't come out of her T-shirt, she'd buy her a new one. Then Priya apologized for calling Gaby a brat.

Even though you are one, she thought.

Belle added, "All right. Let's put this behind us. Your keywords this summer, ladies, are 'kindness' and 'courtesy'. Got it?"

"Yes," Priya said, along with the others.

"You had better all get along, or else," Belle concluded.

Then the circle broke up and everyone got into their beds. In her baby tee and shorts, Priya lay in the bunk above Candace, worn out from all the craziness, but still wired for the same reason. After the most supreme freak-out of her entire summer camp experience, she had no idea how she was going to fall asleep. That, plus wondering who Spence liked better, her or Chelsea...

He can't like Chelsea! That violates all the laws of God and man! Have I wandered into the Bizarro World?

Then Candace whispered, "Priya?"

"Yes?" Priya whispered back.

"Belle said we had to get along 'or else'. Or else what?"

"I don't know," Priya said into the darkness.

CHAPTER FIVE

Morning came way too early, as far as Alyssa was concerned. But Brynn had gotten up already to do some yoga. She claimed yoga helped clear her mind, which helped her with her acting. Alyssa thought she should give it a try too, except she just didn't have the heart for it. The fight had upset her. And Tori's hints about some killer on the loose scared her. She didn't know if she ever wanted to hear the full low-down on that subject.

On the way to the flag-raising, the entire bunk was draggy and awkward around one another. Belle had darker circles under her eyes and she seemed even paler than the day before. She was spooky-looking, and Alyssa kept her distance. The counsellor spent most of her time writing on her clipboard and counting heads as they walked down the hill. She was obsessed with making sure that all eleven of her charges could be accounted for. Her anxiety made Alyssa anxious — Tom Esposito *had* gone home with glandular fever last summer, right?

After the flag was raised, the campers filed into the mess hall for breakfast. Alyssa watched as David bounded up to Jenna. Natalie, Valerie and Simon strolled along together. Alex and Adam were clearly in couple mode. Priya looked wounded as Spence walked with *Chelsea*. What was up with that?

After Adam peeled off to sit with his bunk, Alyssa caught up with Alex.

Alex sighed. "Lyss, what is going *on*? I've been waiting all year for camp and now I'm almost sorry I came."

"Even though you have a boyfriend?" Alyssa asked.

"Even though." Alex sighed.

"I hear you," Alyssa agreed.

"Last night our bunk went psycho," Alex continued.

"Totally psycho," Alyssa concurred.

Brynn and Jordan walked ahead of them, Jordan's head bent towards Brynn's.

"Brynn and Jordan are still tight. That's nice," Alex said. "And I talked Adam out of the three cupcakes he was charging us to give back Tori's stuff."

"Work it, girl," Alyssa urged her with a little wink.

"At least someone's getting along."

But as 5A sat on the two benches at the long wooden breakfast table reserved for them in the mess hall, Brynn squeezed in beside Alyssa.

"Jordan wants to talk to me about something," she said under her breath. "He asked me to meet him during siesta."

"Cool," Alyssa replied as she swallowed down some bug juice.

"I don't know." Brynn leaned her elbows on the table. "When you ask to talk to someone later like that? It's usually something bad. Otherwise you just say what's on your mind right then and there."

"No way. He probably wants to ask you to be his date for the social." Alyssa took another sip of juice. The second sip was no better than the first. "Maybe he's too shy to ask you in public."

"Oh." Brynn's face lost some of its tension. "I hadn't thought of that. Maybe that's it." She grinned at Alyssa. "It's hard to imagine Jordan being shy."

"Who's hungry?" Clarissa asked, carrying a big round tray. Since Clarissa was a CIT, it was her job to act as the bunk's server. Her short blonde hair reminded Alyssa of Tinkerbell. Her well-developed calves and pointy ears just completed the package. She was very cute and perky, even at this early hour. She offered them

Pete's version of French toast, which was pathetic little squares of soggy burned bread. Also, bacon, about two notches past "well done".

And of course, mass quantities of bug juice.

"Is it just me, or is this worse than usual?" Alex murmured across from Alyssa, as she experimentally nibbled on a piece of bacon.

"Everything okay?" Clarissa asked, walking down Alyssa's side of the table.

"Sure, fine," Alyssa assured her. Everyone's heads bobbed. Lie, lie, lie. It would be too complicated to update Clarissa each and every time there was another dip in bunk morale.

Seated at the end of the table, Belle made a note on her clipboard.

All the girls were on their best behaviour through the rest of breakfast. Even Chelsea was quiet, and when she spoke, she was actually polite. Bunk 5A might not have been at war, but they were far away from being a tight bunk, which made Alyssa's heart sink.

At the conclusion of the meal, Belle stood at the end of their table and told them to stay seated because Dr. Steve and Tashya were coming to talk to them. Tashya was the head of the fifth division.

"It's because we went berserk," Jenna muttered.

"*You* went berserk," Gaby sniped.

"Guys, don't," Alyssa pleaded as Dr. Steve and Tashya drew near.

"Good morning, campers," Dr. Steve began.

There were scattered subdued replies.

Alex raised her hand. "Are we in trouble?"

Dr. Steve looked at each girl in turn before he answered.

"Not yet." He crossed his arms over his navy blue Camp Lakeview polo shirt.

Alyssa didn't like the sound of that.

"You may have noticed that a lot of your friends from the fourth division didn't return to camp this summer," he said. "We're not sure why. But those of you who did come back are clearly having problems getting along."

"No kidding," Gaby whispered. Alyssa wanted to kick her. Luckily, Dr. Steve didn't seem to have heard.

"We can't let this kind of situation go on," Dr. Steve continued. "As of today, you are all on probation."

What does that mean? Alyssa wondered as she traded worried glances with Natalie, Brynn and Jenna.

"I would rather send all of you home than perpetuate the bad feelings I'm seeing at Camp

Lakeview," the camp director continued. There was a *big* reaction to that as his words sunk in. Get sent home? This was *huge*.

"I want you to prove to me that you can come together and show me some true Camp Lakeview spirit. Where we treat everyone at camp like a member of our family."

"Some families are very dysfunctional," Gaby muttered.

Dr. Steve looked at Tashya, who took the floor.

"We're going to work on some bonding exercises with you girls," Tashya announced. "And that will start today, when 5A leaves on an overnight nature campout." As the girls began to talk all at once, Tashya raised her hand to signal silence. "All your slots in your electives will be held for you and the auditions for *The Legend of Sleepy Hollow* aren't until next week."

"We'll be leaving after lunch, during siesta," Belle said with a little smile. "Clarissa and I have started planning a really fun adventure for you. I hope no one peeked at my clipboard yesterday."

Oh. That's why she's so into her clipboard!

Alyssa glanced over at Valerie as the light went on in the other girl's eyes too. That must have been what Belle had been hiding from her. So they had already been planning a trip before the bunk went berserko.

87

Dr. Steve said, "I really need to see some improvement in your behaviour. Please believe me when I tell you that I'm serious about this."

He looked at Belle. "It would be very painful for your counsellor to report any bad behaviour on this overnight, but I've asked her to be honest about how it goes. She's agreed to let me know if she thinks any of you need to be sent home."

Alyssa swallowed hard and nodded when his gaze rested on her. Then she heard Chelsea mutter, "There's no one *at* my home."

After the meeting, the group returned to the cabin to perform their chores. Each girl snapped to. There was no playful arguing or complaining over who had bathroom duty. After the sinks, toilets and shower stalls sparkled, all the beds were made, and the floor was swept clean, they got their gear ready for the overnight and helped carry it down to the parking lot. There were no smiles. There was a lot of trudging. Going on an overnight together was clearly the last thing anyone wanted to do.

To make matters worse, lunch was tuna surprise.

Natalie groaned. "No! No! I can't stand tuna surprise! Throw the tuna back into the lake!"

The whole bunk laughed, all in fun. It was the first light-hearted moment they had shared since the meeting with Dr. Steve.

"Here we are," Clarissa announced, carrying her large brown tray topped with a steaming bowl of the wretched casserole. "Who's hungry?"

"Natalie Goode is starving. Give it all to Nat!" Jenna cried. "Tuna surprise is her favouritest thing in the world."

Everyone cracked up and Clarissa chuckled as she sailed to the end of the bench to serve Natalie first.

"Give her a doggy bag for the bus too. She can't get enough of it," Tori called after Clarissa.

"Ha-ha," Natalie said. "Lucky thing I have plenty of PowerBars to see me through." Then she blanched. "I forgot to pack them!"

"You're going to have to rough it like the rest of us," Valerie informed her. "Hot dogs and hamburgers all the way."

"Except for the tofu hot dogs I packed," Alyssa said. She was a vegetarian.

"Yuckorama." Jenna crossed her eyes. "I'd rather have tuna surprise three times a day for the rest of the summer!"

"Tofu hot dogs are great," Tori said. "My friend Kallista and I get them all the time."

"Eww, eww, eww." Jenna shook her head. "There's no accounting for taste."

"Right," Chelsea jumped in. "Sometimes you just wonder how someone can like something...or some*one*." She flashed a superior grin at Priya.

"That's right. You just wonder," Priya retorted.

"Girls, cut it! Nix on the smackdown!" Valerie cried.

"Guys, probation, remember?" Alyssa reminded them in a hushed voice.

"Dr. Steve wouldn't send any of us home," Gaby insisted. "They'd have to return our camp fees."

"Maybe he doesn't have to give back our fees," Alyssa said. "Maybe there's something in our registration papers that says if they have to send us home because we misbehaved, Camp Lakeview gets to keep the money."

Gaby blinked as if she hadn't thought of that. "Well, they wouldn't do that to all of us. Eleven campers sent home? They would get bad publicity."

"You heard Dr. Steve," Alyssa argued. "They've already had some bad publicity or something. So many girls our age didn't come back."

"Maybe they heard about Cropsy too," Tori said.

"Cropsy again!" Gaby made a fist and lightly banged

90

the table with it. "Either tell us the whole story or stop talking about it!"

"I'll tell you tonight," Tori promised.

During siesta, 5A climbed aboard the bus. As they prepared to leave, Brynn paused on the steps and gazed over the landscape. Her stomach fluttered and she sighed.

"Afraid you'll never see it again, *mwahaha*?" Jenna teased her. "Goodbye, Camp Lakeview. We who are about to die salute you!"

But of course that wasn't it. Brynn didn't think they were going to die on a camp-sponsored overnight. But it did feel almost as dire. The thing was, she was going to have to leave without talking to Jordan.

Brynn sat beside Priya on the bus. "Tell me the truth, Priya. Do you know why Jordan wanted to meet up with me during siesta?"

Priya crossed her forefingers and held them up, as if to ward off the evil eye. "Brynn, please don't ask me to get between you two this summer. It makes Jordan and me fight. Besides," she added before Brynn could say anything, "he didn't tell me."

"But...has he said anything lately about us?" Brynn asked. She shrugged. "He hasn't been hanging out with me as much as I thought he would."

"No, he hasn't said anything," Priya said. "And he hasn't said anything because I gave him the same rule. No speak-y." Then she softened a little and added, "Although he breaks it all the time to tell me that he really, really likes you."

Brynn's face broke into a huge smile. "Really?"

"Argh." Priya rolled her eyes.

"Sorry," Brynn said, not really very sorry. "But... really?"

"We are camping *in the forest*?"

Tori sat two seats behind Bob the driver, pressing her hands against the window frame as the bus zoomed off the main highway and onto a narrow, two-lane road. It was lined with pine trees, straight as sentries, their lush boughs concealing all kinds of great hiding places for insane knife-wielding criminals.

"Not liking this, either," Brynn murmured beside Priya.

Priya raised a brow. "Brynn, be serious. Tori's little hints about this Cropsy guy don't really scare you, do they?"

Brynn wrinkled her nose. "Kind of," she admitted.

Priya shook her head. "Think about it. First of all,

have you ever heard about an insane psycho killer around here?"

"Pree, four years ago, I had never heard about a summer camp around here," Brynn said.

Just then, Jenna slid from her place with Candace across the aisle into the seat in front of Priya and Brynn.

"I am seriously worried about Candace," she announced in a whisper.

"Oh?" Brynn and Priya glanced discreetly at Jenna's seatmate, whose head was ducked down as she read a book and busily gnawed on her thumbnail.

"She's worried about the lions," Jenna deadpanned.

"No way," Priya said.

Jenna nodded.

"Jordan, you are a dead man," Priya murmured, trying to hide her smile. "Allow me," she said to Jenna.

Then she scooted around Brynn and sat beside Candace across the aisle. Thinking of Jordan's nutty story about the escaped circus lions, Brynn grew pensive as they rode along, the bus passing into shade as it rolled through the tunnel of pines. As she wondered what Jordan had wanted to discuss, the temperature dropped, a momentary break from the oppressive, moist heat.

"I'm going to need some serious help out here in the wilderness," Jenna said. Brynn raised her brows, giving Jenna her full attention. "The possibilities for pranking are so endless. It's going to be hard to behave, and I really *need* to behave."

Brynn smiled fondly at her old friend. "I totally get that," she said. "Just fight it, Jenna."

"I'm trying," Jenna gasped in a husky voice. She made her hands shake. "Must...not...prank...pranking... bad..."

They giggled together. Jenna paused. Then she muttered the word *lion* under her breath.

"Don't make fun," Brynn admonished her. She gazed out the window. "*I'm* thinking about all those slasher movies I wish I had never watched."

"Adam has the world's most extensive collection of gore-fest flicks," Jenna said, nodding. "All I have to say is that I am really, really, really glad the boys didn't come with us. They would be merciless. They would think scaring us to death would be a totally awesome bonding experience."

"Boys," Brynn said.

"Boys," Jenna agreed. "We should set Cropsy on them."

"If we knew who Cropsy was," Brynn added.

* * *

They rode along for what seemed like for ever. The sky began to darken.

"Was that thunder?" Candace called out, her voice high-pitched and nervous. Priya, who was still sitting with her, gave her a pat.

The bus rolled onto a rickety-looking wooden bridge and Brynn gazed down at the dark water. Shadow Lake was well named; mysterious swirls of black and grey rippled, formed and re-formed.

As she stared down into the eddies and currents, she thought she saw a grey, whispery mist waft above the surface.

"You guys know the story of the Headless Horseman, right?" Gaby piped up. "How he came after Ichabod Crane on a bridge *just like the one we're on now?*"

"And he threw a flaming pumpkin right at Ichabod!" Natalie said from across the aisle, doing a pantomime of someone throwing something over their head with both hands.

"Are you auditioning for Katrina too, Brynn?" Natalie asked her. Natalie hopped up from her original seat and plopped down behind her, even though they weren't supposed to move around on the bus. "Because if you do, I don't have a *ghost* of a chance."

Brynn pretend-bopped Natalie on the head. "Bad pun, bad," she chastised her.

"I have to say, the play selection surprises me," Belle said. "I mean, I'm new to Camp Lakeview, but I was looking over the list of productions the camp has put on in the past. You usually do something light and fun. Last year was *Annie*."

"You should have been here the year we did *The Texas Chainsaw Massacre*," Jenna said. She mimicked holding up a chainsaw and yanking on the starter. Then she let 'er rip.

"Jenna Bloom, it's not nice to try to fool the counsellor," Belle said, wagging a finger at Jenna. Alex, Natalie, Tori and Valerie broke into guffaws, and some of the tension in the bus dissipated.

Then thunder really did rumble. The laughter died down and Belle turned to the window, studying the sky.

Natalie and Brynn traded looks. Natalie murmured, "Maybe they want us to camp in the rain. So we'll start melting and bond better."

Brynn pondered that, scratching her cheek as she studied their counsellor. In the dim light, Belle's eyes were invisible in their dark sockets.

"I'm kind of freaked that we'll be out in the wilderness with her," Brynn said. "She's so pale."

"Like a vampire," Natalie concurred, turning to gaze at Belle as well. "Isn't this the way those movies

96

always start? The two friends noticing the problem and everyone else is all tra-la-la, until it's too late?"

"Everyone else is not all tra-la-la," Brynn pointed out. "We're all pretty tense-tense-tense."

"Well, being told that if we *don't* get all tra-la-la, we'll be sent home..." Natalie leaned her head against her seat back and stared up at the ceiling. Her neck cricked. "Not the most relaxing way to live."

They left the bridge. The pines grew thicker together, shrouding the bus in deeper shadow. Brynn put on her sweatshirt. A few minutes later, Bob downshifted, causing the gears to grind for a second or two, which made Brynn wince. Belle spoke to him a moment, then got to her feet and faced the girls.

"We're almost there," she said. "Start gathering up your stuff."

CHAPTER SIX

About five minutes later, the bus trundled down a gravel incline, rolling to a stop a few metres above a cleared area bookended by pine trees and large granite boulders. The boulders were covered with graffiti, attesting to the fact that this was a popular place to camp – and not some completely cut-off no-man's-land. There were some bushes beside the boulders and a drooping pine tree that looked as if lightning had cracked it.

Directly in front of the campsite, there was a concrete fire ring as wide across as Chelsea was tall. There were two picnic tables, one on either side of the fire ring. Beyond it, the ground sloped downwards towards Shadow Lake. The trees were thinner, revealing darkened silver slices of the lake. The sun peered through the branches and sparkled on the water. Some ducks took flight, quacking as they rose into the air.

"Check it out, Nat," Tori said, gesturing with her

head towards the lake as she helped unroll one of the tarps that would serve as a floor mat for the tents. "Supernature-rama."

"Super*natural*-rama," Natalie replied, placing two sleeping bags beside a growing pile of camping supplies. She daintily wiped her hands on her turquoise shorts. "This place reminds me of the location of about a dozen low-budget horror movies my dad was in when he was starting out as an actor."

"Michael's dad, too," Tori said as she smoothed the tarp.

Chelsea knew Tori was dating the actor Cameron Stevenson's son. Chelsea couldn't imagine the kind of life Tori led. To be so rich and pretty, and hanging out with superstars and going to movie premieres. Natalie, whose dad was another superstar actor, seemed to have a charmed life as well. She had a totally glamorous mom who also spent half her time travelling all over the world, buying art. Natalie went to a private school.

Just like Chelsea used to.

Don't be such a downer, she told herself. *Maybe the girls in the bunk are their typical unfriendly selves, but Spence might like you. That's pretty cool.*

Except that she knew that Spence had started liking Priya last summer, and Chelsea figured they had been e-mailing each other ever since. Maybe even visiting each other. So Spence was supposed to be off-limits. She knew the rules of girls, even if she had never played the game before.

No boy has ever talked to me and hung around me like Spence, she thought. *And besides, Priya totally does not deserve him. She's mean to me. They all are.*

She had really, really wanted camp to be so much fun that she could just forget about what was going on in her world back home. But it wasn't turning out that way, and all the pressure and the worry had already popped out at the worst possible moments. Last night she'd done stuff that had gotten the whole bunk in trouble. She *had* pushed Gaby. She just hadn't admitted it. She felt awful...and that just added to her pressure.

As she tried to decide where on the crowded tables to set the box she was holding, she brushed past Alex, who slid a glance towards Alyssa. None of these girls had a clue what she was going through. And what really hurt was that they *should* have a clue. They knew her dad was really sick. They fussed over Alex and her diabetes all the time, but no one had even *asked* Chelsea how her father was doing.

A year and a half ago they had given her a journal they made to let her know they cared...and then they went back to being their mean, snotty, excluding selves, posting to one another on the blog, and inviting one another to things that she never got invited to...

"I'm so jazzed. When I get home, Michael and I are going to this benefit dinner at this new restaurant his dad's opening. I got such an awesome dress for it," Tori told Natalie.

"When I come to LA during winter break, we'll have to go there." Natalie waggled her brows. "So *I'll* need an awesome dress too."

Chelsea walked stiffly past them. Her most recent shopping expedition had been for socks and underwear for camp. Nothing else new, not even a new pair of sneakers.

As she bent over to set down the box, she tripped on a flipped-over end of the tarp and lost her grip. The box crashed to the ground.

"Chelsea, please be careful," Belle snapped as she dodged around Chelsea with *two* boxes in her arms.

Tears stung Chelsea's eyes. She choked out, "Sorry," but in such a low voice even she couldn't hear herself.

She has the power to send you home.

Chelsea took a deep breath, licked her lips, and raised her chin. "I'm sorry," she repeated in a louder voice.

"Okay, thank you."

Belle bent down and lowered her burden to the ground with what seemed like exaggerated care, as if she was demonstrating to Chelsea how to do it. As if Chelsea was a moron.

Chelsea turned back around to get another load. She caught sight of Jenna rolling her eyes at Alex. The two girls sat cross-legged on the ground. They were supposed to be reading the directions for erecting the tents. But it was obvious to Chelsea that they were just goofing off – and making fun of her.

She balled her fists, but she didn't say anything, just went straight back to the bus to get another load.

Once the bus was emptied, Bob gave them a wave.

"You girls be on your guard out here tonight. You don't want the boogeyman to get you." He laughed to himself, and backed out until he could turn around. Then he disappeared down the road.

Candace looked longingly after him. Chelsea wanted to comfort her and tell her everything was going to be all right. But she didn't know how to say that without fibbing a little – because sometimes things didn't turn out all right.

"You can be in my tent tonight," Chelsea told her.

"Oh." Candace flushed and cleared her throat. "Thanks," she said, unenthusiastically, and Chelsea understood: Candace didn't *want* to be in her tent.

"It'll be Tori, Nat and Alyssa, together again," Natalie said as she threaded the poles of one of the tents through the tabs on the side.

"We're going to draw lots for the sleeping arrangements," Belle announced. "In fact, let's do that right now. I've put all your names on pieces of paper." She held up strips of paper from her notebook and dumped them into Chelsea's emptied condiment box.

Chelsea wound up with Jenna, Tori and Candace. Natalie, Alex and Gaby were in another tent. Brynn was with Priya, Valerie and Alyssa. At least Chelsea wasn't with Gaby. She had thought they were going to be best friends this summer, but it sure wasn't turning out that way. She wondered how Tori, Alyssa and Natalie felt about being separated. They were usually a tight threesome. And she wondered how unhappy Jenna, Tori and Candace were that they had to share a tent with her.

After they organized their tents, Belle told them they could go swimming in the lake. Eager to get some relief from the heat, the girls raced to put on their suits.

As she changed into last year's black and white tankini, something about her camping gear bothered Chelsea, but she couldn't figure out what it was. She glanced suspiciously at the others, wondering if someone had done something to her stuff.

"Stay in my range," Belle ordered them. "And swim with a buddy. Absolutely no swimming off alone."

The group reached the water's edge, which was sandy in some places and covered with pebbles in others. Dropping their towels along the shoreline, Jenna, Brynn and Alex darted right in.

"It's freezing!" Jenna whooped.

Natalie and Tori sat on the shore, while Brynn and Alex started up a water fight. The bunk was pairing up in twos and threes, and Chelsea quickly calculated that no one was waiting up for her.

So she turned around with the thought of heading back to the campsite. But she realized that if she went back alone, Belle would be all over her, asking her why she wasn't hanging out with the bunk. She wouldn't be showing proper 5A team spirit.

Frustrated and uncertain, she turned back around and looked at the girls, most of whom were waist-deep in the water, laughing and dodging vigorous splashes. Even Candace, who was so shy, was bobbing up to her shoulders and laughing.

No one called to her, urging her to join in the fun.

Probably because they're glad to be rid of me, Chelsea thought.

She hovered at the shoreline, acting as if she had decided not to go in, but was still happy to be there.

She bent and picked up a rock shaped a little like an arrowhead, then dropped it back down.

The girls kept on with their water fight. Chelsea's mind wandered to thoughts of her parents. She missed them. She wanted to know how things were going in DC. She couldn't wait until Sunday, when she could e-mail her mom and dad from Dr. Steve's office.

A bird cawed. Something made ripples in the lake — probably a fish. She heard frogs and crickets.

And...*music*. There. The faintest hint of a melody made her cock her head. It was either very low, or very far away.

Then it was gone.

She looked up and down the shoreline to see if anyone besides 5A was there — a fisherman, maybe, or some other campers. But there was no one. She began to wonder if she had heard anything at all. Maybe she had just imagined it. It had been very faint. Maybe Belle had brought a radio.

The sun beat down, and Chelsea was sweating. She walked down to the water, unlaced her tennis shoes, and took an experimental step in. She was kind of far away from the others, but she really wasn't in the mood to hang out with them.

She went in up to her knees, and then her waist, and she dipped her head back into the frigid water. For the first time in a long time, she let the tears flow. Weeping, she lay on her back and floated, trying to calm down by taking deep breaths.

"Chelsea!" Belle shouted.

Chelsea jerked and splashed water on her face to hide the fact that she'd been crying. Then she turned around and faced Belle. Her counsellor was standing about three metres away in a black one-piece. Her entire body from head to toe was white, except for her cheeks, which were bright red. Wow, she was really mad.

"I told you girls to stay where I could see you," she said. "And you're all the way over here. *And* you don't have a swim buddy."

Startled, Chelsea moved in a little circle, taking stock of her surroundings. She was stunned to realize that she had drifted so far away. In fact, the girls were little dots up the shore. She wilted. She was so busted. She hadn't meant to do anything wrong.

"I'm sorry," she said, and she meant it. "I got distracted."

"Please get out now," Belle said. "And I'll gather the others. We're going back to camp to start dinner."

Chelsea swallowed hard and slogged back to shore. Belle waited with her hands on her hips, as if she didn't quite trust Chelsea to do as she asked.

When they reached the campsite, the other girls laughed and cracked jokes as they changed back into their clothes. They seemed relaxed and happy. Chelsea got dressed in miserable silence. Belle's anger stung her.

After everyone was clothed, Belle explained that part of their bonding experience included making dinner together. She and Clarissa would supervise building and lighting the fire, but for the rest of it, the girls were on their own. Meanwhile, Belle and Clarissa would finish working on their "adventure".

"The 5A Challenge," Belle finished. "A really awesome scavenger hunt!"

"Cool!" Alex cheered, and all the other girls started nodding and laughing excitedly. Chelsea tried to muster up a smile, but she couldn't. The last thing on earth she wanted to do was go on a scavenger hunt. She just wanted to sit down and cry.

Making dinner was a brand-new nightmare. Every time Chelsea tried to help, one of the other girls would take over her chore and make it her own. She kept finding herself pushed out of the way as someone would say, "Excuse me, that's okay, I've got it." First it was helping to gather firewood, then assisting Alyssa, Belle and

Clarissa as they built the fire in the concrete fire ring.

"No, Chelsea. Not that way, Chelsea," it seemed like the counsellor and CIT were saying at every moment. And Alyssa kept saying, "That's not the way we learned it last year."

"Okay, fine," Chelsea said as Alyssa rearranged her starter wood into a tighter triangle. She tried not to sound irritated, but it was hard.

Then they unpacked three hamburger grillers and Belle selected Natalie, Alex and Valerie to cook the hamburgers while she supervised. Chelsea thought it would be way cooler to let each girl grill her own burger, but she didn't say anything. She didn't want to be told that she couldn't do it because she was too much of a loser.

Fuming in silence, Chelsea looked for something else to do. She decided to neaten up the collection of squeeze bottles of ketchup, mayonnaise, mustard, barbecue sauce and pickle relish on one of the picnic tables, but as she got to work, she accidentally dropped the ketchup bottle on top of the tomatoes Alex was slicing.

"Oh, I'm sorry, Alex," Chelsea said, reaching for the ketchup bottle.

"Argh! Shoo! Scat!" Alex said, and even though Chelsea could hear the teasing lilt in her voice, she started to lose it. But she didn't let anyone see the tears welling in her eyes. They would just make fun of her. If she were anyone else, they would be all worried about hurt feelings and gather around the person and try to show her support. But they'd just roll their eyes and snicker if it was Chelsea.

Dinner was served at last. They ate off paper plates, but there were a few utensils and the hamburger grillers to clean. Belle looked around at everyone.

"Chelsea, I don't think you've had a chore yet. You can do the dishes."

Chelsea was mortified. *Had a chore* yet? She felt as if Belle was calling her a slacker. She must not have noticed all the times Chelsea had attempted to pitch in.

"Okay." Chelsea bit her tongue. She got out the water they had brought up from the lake and heated it over the fire in their kettle. Then she poured in some sanitizer.

"I'll dry," Clarissa offered, but Belle shook her head.

"The girls are supposed to do it all. Besides, we still have a few more scavenger hunt clues to work out."

So no one dried. No one else, that is. By the time Chelsea was done, everyone else had arranged things in their tents and unrolled their sleeping bags. She discovered that she had been put closest to the tent flap, for everyone to step on all night as they went in and out of the tent to go to the bathroom.

The others had on their pyjamas by the time Chelsea went to look for her pjs inside her pack. She came up empty. She had brought a towel, her bathing suit and her toothbrush. But there was no change of clothes, not even socks or underwear.

She sat back on her heels, perplexed, until she mentally retraced her actions before they had left on the bus. She couldn't remember packing pjs or extra clothes. She was so distracted, worrying about getting sent home and listening to Gaby ranting about how unfair it was that they were being forced to go on an overnight with "these people". Chelsea knew everyone had turned her and Gaby into the bad guys of the bunk and she was trying to figure out how to change that...

...and then Belle had asked everyone to think of some songs to sing tonight at their campfire...

And I guess I forgot to finish packing, she thought. *Great. Just great. My socks are filthy and my clothes stink.*

Huffing, she closed up her pack and joined the others around the fire ring. They were roasting marshmallows in their cute pyjamas. They looked like they were in some kind of fun commercial for Skittles or Coke Zero.

On the left-hand picnic table, a propane lantern hissed, and bugs fluttered against the glass. There were bugs everywhere, and Chelsea went back to her tent to retrieve her insect repellent. *That*, at least, she had remembered.

She unzipped the flap.

"Hey," Alex said, glancing up at her with a startled look on her face.

Just as she realized she had gone to the wrong tent, Chelsea looked down at Alex. Alex had all her diabetes stuff out – her little needles and the finger stick thing that she used to check her blood sugar levels.

"Sorry," Chelsea muttered. Her hands trembled; in her mind's eye, she saw a nurse giving her father a shot of the new cancer drug. And even though it didn't make sense, she got mad at Alex for being sick. She didn't want anyone to be sick. She didn't want anyone to have any problems.

Distressed, she turned around and headed back to the logs around the fire ring. She sat down in the first empty space...right next to Jenna, who, of course, had remembered *her* cotton drawstring jammie bottoms and a Camp Lakeview T-shirt. Just as Chelsea settled in her space, Jenna turned to see who was sitting next to her. When she saw that it was Chelsea, she jerked as if she had just seen a monster.

Great, Chelsea thought again. She slapped a mosquito as it landed on her arm. Then a second one pricked her cheek.

She looked longingly over at the quartet of tents where her repellent was. Belle and Clarissa were standing in front of their tent, counting off paces and writing down notes. Then Alex emerged from her tent and approached the fire ring. She made a point of looking away from Chelsea and Chelsea felt even worse.

"Aren't you going to change into your pjs?" Candace asked Chelsea as she sat on the log section beside her.

Chelsea shrugged. "Not right now," she said. Which was stupid, because it wasn't as if she was going to be able to change later.

"Okay, now we're going to sing some songs and have s'mores," Belle announced.

She and Clarissa passed out marshmallows, skewers, pieces of Hershey's chocolate bars and graham crackers. She divided the girls into two groups to toast their marshmallows. Gaby was in the first group and Chelsea was in the second, and Chelsea was relieved that they'd been split up. Candace kind of hung out with her and Chelsea was really grateful.

They sang some camp songs, including "Bug Juice" and "Bubblegum", and a few more current songs. Once everyone grew hoarse from singing at the top of their lungs, they played "Operator", cracking up at how mangled the words and phrases got as they moved through the raspy telephone line.

Then Tori whispered with Belle, who nodded and handed over her extra-long, super-bright black flashlight. Tori walked behind the flickering fire ring and clicked the flashlight on, holding it beneath her chin. The brilliant upswept light cast dark shadows over her features, and she looked way creepy.

"Now I will tell you the story of Cropsy," Tori announced. Her voice was hoarse and raspy.

"Finally," Jenna called out. Only it came out in a squeak. She was hoarse too, from all the extra-loud singing.

"Don't make it too scary!" Brynn gravelled out.

"Okay, wait a minute," Belle said, as she pushed a roasted marshmallow onto a graham cracker covered with a layer of chocolate squares. Ghostly white, her eyes like two empty sockets, she looked hard at Tori. "I thought you said *everyone* wanted to hear this."

"We do," Brynn whispered loudly. "Just if it's not too scary!"

"You totally love all the drama, don't you," Gaby said in a similarly breathy voice. "C'mon, just let her tell it. It's getting late and it's probably a dumb story anyway."

"Gaby, please be nice," Belle reminded her. "Brynn, if you're sure…"

"It's okay." Brynn raised her chin as if she were mustering all her courage. "Go for it, Tori."

Tori cleared her throat. "This is the true story of Cropsy, the crazed killer of Shadow Lake."

"Many years ago, a boys' bunk was camping in the forest by Shadow Lake, which is the lake Camp Lakeview is named for. They were all settled in, listening to the radio, when a news bulletin came on. An inmate had just escaped from the nearby Asylum for the Criminally Insane. His name was Cropsy.

"Cropsy had been locked up six years before, and he was so violent and crazy that he had to be kept in a straitjacket in a padded room, all by himself. They slid his meals through a little slot in the door while a guard trained a gun on him.

"'Everyone must clear the area at once!' the radio announcer continued. 'Until Cropsy is apprehended, anyone in the forest is in terrible danger!'

"So the boys broke camp as fast as they could. They rolled up their sleeping bags and loaded up their backpacks. After their counsellor put out their fire and passed out flashlights, he told them that they would head out of the woods and make for the highway, where they would flag someone down. If they couldn't get enough rides for everyone, they'd at least get the driver to notify the Pennsylvania State Troopers that they were there.

"But as they left their campsite, a strange fog rolled in off the lake. It was so thick that the boys couldn't see one another. They couldn't see the beams of their flashlights, even. They could only hear one another's voices.

"So this one guy named Randy kept hearing someone calling his name, and he kept following the voice. He thought he recognized it. He thought it was his counsellor's voice. He trained his flashlight on the fog and he thought he saw a figure walking in front of it – like a shadow on the billowing white mist.

"After a while, he couldn't see the figure. He stopped walking and angled his flashlight up, down, to the left, and to the right. He couldn't see anything but the fog.

"He listened for the voice. Any voice. Anything. He didn't know what to do. He didn't know where his bunk was. He didn't know where he was.

"Then he heard the voice again: 'Raaaannndyyyy, come to me.'

"He was sure it was his counsellor, but he couldn't

tell what direction it was coming from. He walked straight ahead and crashed into something hard!

"It was only a tree trunk.

"He backed away, tripping over something on the ground. He dropped to his knees and felt it. It was rough and spindly, and he thought it must be a tree root.

"'Hello?' he called out.

"'Raaaannndyyyy, come to meeeee.'

"He got to his feet.

"'Where are you?' he said.

"'Close. Very close.'

"A twig snapped right behind him! Then strange, high-pitched giggling started right in his ear, and Randy suddenly knew that the man behind him was not his counsellor. It was Cropsy!"

"No, no more!" Brynn blurted. "I'm too freaked out!"

"Time-out. Enough." Belle gestured to Tori. "If Brynn's too scared, we should stop."

Tori flicked off the flashlight and lowered it to her side.

Oh, for heaven's sake, Chelsea thought, but she kept her mouth shut. She wanted to hear the end. From the looks on everyone else's faces, they did too.

"Crop-sy, Crop-sy, Crop-sy," Natalie and Jenna

chanted, clapping their hands and laughing at each other's scratchy voices.

"Tell it, sister," Valerie squawked. A couple of the other girls cackled like witches.

Brynn theatrically fanned her face. "Belle, it's all right. I just felt the need for a dramatic pause. For the good of the bunk, I'll endure this terrifying tale."

Chelsea rolled her eyes. Gaby saw her do it, and shook her head tiredly as if to say, *Can you believe this drama queen?*

"Hmmm," Belle considered.

"Look, if I get too scared, I'll go hide in my tent," Brynn promised. *"Please* let Tori finish."

Just then, Clarissa came over to Belle and they talked for a few seconds. Belle stood up.

"I'm going to be over by the tents with Clarissa," she told the girls. "We need to check some things for tomorrow's scavenger hunt. If *any* of you want Tori to stop, all you have to do is speak up. And if you need us, we'll be right over there." She pointed to the cluster of tents. "Okay?"

The girls nodded.

"I'm good. Honest," Brynn rasped.

Tori waited while Belle left the campfire. Then she flicked the flashlight back on and positioned it beneath her chin.

* * *

Crouched on the road behind some bushes, Dan elbowed Jeremiah as they spied on the summer camp girls below them. Of course, Jeremiah only had eyes for Clarissa. She was so pretty.

Dan was disgusted. "Dude," he whispered, "that is totally the wrong story! Where did she hear that? Cropsy didn't escape from an insane asylum."

"Shut up," Jeremiah whispered back. "If they hear us, they'll freak out."

Dan's eyes glinted in the moonlight. "Well, you said Clarissa likes to be scared. So let's scare her."

Jeremiah hesitated. Dan elbowed him again. "Come on, Jer, just for fun. Just a little bit. Then we'll let 'em know it's just us."

"I don't know," Jeremiah said.

"That way you can see her," Dan went on. "And then you can invite them to have ice cream tomorrow on their way back to camp, to make up for pranking them. So you'll get to see her twice in two days."

Jeremiah quirked a grin at Dan. "You're devious, dude. Okay. Let's scare them. I'll pretend I'm Cropsy." He opened his mouth to call out in a spooky voice.

"Wait. Let's go get the chainsaw out of the truck," Dan suggested. "We can use it as a prop. We'll put on the Camp Lakeview Chainsaw Massacre!"

"The chainsaw? I don't know," Jeremiah said. "That's pretty extreme."

"She'll love it," Dan promised. "Trust me."

The two crept away, down the road, towards Dan's truck.

"Okay, we left off with Randy hearing the giggling behind him," Tori reminded her rapt audience.

"Randy jumped backwards...but he fell over the hard, gnarled thing again. He slammed onto his back and the breath was knocked out of him.

"The giggling grew louder and louder. Then bony fingers wrapped around his neck and started to squeeze. He smelled something awful, like rotten meat. It was the breath of his attacker.

"Randy kicked and flailed his arms, but it was no use. The hands around his neck grew tighter and tighter, until he passed out.

"When he woke up, he discovered that he was handcuffed to a brick wall. He was in a basement, and a rat was sitting on top of his foot, squeaking at him. Then there was a jingling noise, followed by heavy footsteps on wood. Through a small window above his head, the moonlight shone on a flight of wooden stairs five metres away.

"Heavy leather boots stomped down the stairs.

"Then legs.

"Then long, bony white fingers, carrying a large ring of keys. That was what was making the jingling sound.

"Randy tried to speak. It was only then that he realized he had been gagged. His eyes bulged above the cloth stretched across the lower half of his face.

"Then...

"...he beheld the face of Cropsy.

"His skin was pulled so tightly across the bones, and it was so thin, that his face looked like a skull. A long, jagged, purple scar ran from his left temple across his nose to the corner of his mouth. He had only one eye. The other eye was covered by a black leather patch.

"'They said I would never leave that asylum alive. But I planned my escape for six long years. And now I'm free!'

"Then he reached into the shadows and pulled out a razor-sharp axe. Randy began to struggle and whimper. Cropsy laughed his crazy laugh and leaned towards him. Closer, closer.

"The moonlight glistened on the axe blade as Cropsy pressed it against Randy's throat.

"Randy struggled harder. He was fighting for his life! And suddenly, his right hand slipped right out of the handcuff! He made a fist and slammed it into

Cropsy's face. Cropsy howled with fury and started to hack across Randy's throat. But Randy grabbed his wrist and deflected the blade. And before he realized what was happening, he cut off Cropsy's arm!

"Cropsy collapsed in a pool of blood. His eyes went wide and unfocused and he gazed up at the ceiling. He made no sound, and he lay still as death.

"Shaking, knowing that he had just escaped the clutches of a madman, yet horrified that he had taken a human life, Randy grabbed the keys. He was trembling so badly that it was difficult for him to unlock the other handcuff around his left wrist. Twice he had to stop to wipe the sweat out of his eyes. He was crying with fear.

"Cropsy didn't move.

"Finally, he unlocked the other handcuff. The cuffs dropped to the concrete floor with a clink.

"Cropsy jerked and lunged for Randy's ankle! Randy screamed, leaping out of his reach.

"Cropsy lunged again, his fingertips grazing Randy's shin.

"Randy kicked at him as he bent down, grabbed the axe, and raced for the stairs. He heard Cropsy grunting as if he were trying to stand up.

"Randy took the stairs two by two until he got to the main floor of a filthy, deserted shack. Rats squeaked as they scurried out of his way.

"Then he saw the dead body of his camp counsellor, laid out on the floor! His head had been cut off and it was sitting on the dead counsellor's chest, grinning at Randy like a Halloween pumpkin! And so were the heads of all his bunkmates! Their bodies were laid out in a row, each with his head on his chest!

"Randy screamed for all he was worth. He flew out of there as fast as he could go, dashing right into the screen door and ripping it off the hinges.

"Beneath the light of the full moon, he raced down to the edge of Shadow Lake. It was covered with fog, rising off of it like thick, choking smoke.

"There was a boat at the water's edge. Without a moment's hesitation, Randy leaped into it and shoved off. There was no paddle, so he decided to use the axe in his hand.

"But it wasn't the axe! To his horror, he discovered that he had grabbed up Cropsy's dismembered arm instead! It was dripping with blood and the fingers clawed at him, trying to dig into his wrist.

"Randy yelled and dropped the arm back into the boat. But it started crawling towards his ankle, inching along. Blood was spurting everywhere, filling up the bottom of the boat. There was so much blood that the boat began to sink.

"Then he heard a horrible wailing behind him. It was

so terrible that Randy was paralysed with fright. He fought to breathe or move his foot as the arm crept towards it.

"The wailing came closer.

"Randy still couldn't move.

"CLOSER!

"Finally he managed to force himself to look, and what he saw froze his blood.

"It was Cropsy!

"The criminally insane, one-armed monster was staggering out of the shack. He was bleeding like crazy from the stump of his right arm. In the moonlight, the blood looked like a geyser of black ooze.

"In his left hand, he was carrying his axe.

"Cropsy raised the axe over his head and howled, 'Give me back my arm!'

"Then from the bottom of the boat, Cropsy's dismembered arm flew at Randy! It grabbed him around the throat and started choking him!

"Cropsy's voice boomed across the lake:

"'I WANT MY ARM!'

"And the gory, bleeding arm dragged Randy out of the boat, through the water, and onto the shore, where Cropsy was waiting for him. His silhouette was carved into the moon as he raised up that axe and WHAM! He cut off Randy's arm!

"Randy was never heard from or seen again.

"And every six years, it happens again. Cropsy hunts down an unsuspecting camper and cuts off his arm. Or *her* arm. And I know this is true because he almost did it to my cousin Nicole's bunkmate's cousin, Samantha, six years ago. Sam went into the woods to pee and she heard Cropsy crashing through the trees, yelling, 'I WANT MY ARM!'

"She flew out of there back to camp, barely escaping with her life. She was so scared that part of her hair turned white. And it's still white!

"But the next morning, one of the other girls in the bunk was missing. Sam asked the counsellor where the girl was, and the counsellor acted very strangely.

"'Oh, Theresa got sick in the night and we had to take her to the hospital,' the counsellor told the bunk. 'Her parents met us there and took her home.'

"No one believed that, of course. No one saw the girl leave. No one ever heard from or saw that girl again. Because Cropsy got her.

"And now...it's been six years since then. And Cropsy is in the woods, searching for a new victim. And when he finds her, he'll cut off her arm and she'll die a terrible, hideous death!"

*   *   *

"And then the circus lions will eat her!" Jenna squeaked as loudly as she could, and the girls screamed.

Priya burst into a fit of uncontrollable laughter. She was honking like a goose. Brynn joined in, shaking her fist at Jenna.

"Fight it! Fight the urge to prank!"

"*What* are you talking about?" Chelsea demanded.

Then Jenna saw Candace's eyes widen and glint with tears, and she realized Candace thought she was making fun of her. *This is why you don't prank any more, Bloom.*

She darted over to Candace and in her haste, accidentally stepped hard on Chelsea's foot.

"Sorry," she said, her attention on Candace.

"*Ow,*" Chelsea grunted.

"Sorry," Jenna said again. She squatted beside Candace, who wouldn't look at her. "Candace, I'm sorry."

"What's all that about lions?" Chelsea was making a huge deal out of rubbing her foot. Demanding all the attention, when it was really Candace whom Jenna had wounded.

"Didn't you hear Jordan at the cookout?" Jenna croaked impatiently. Chelsea shook her head. "Long story. And it wasn't part of *this* story."

"Well, it's a *stupid* story anyway." Chelsea rubbed her foot harder. "And it's bogus. If that's the dark secret of Camp Lakeview, it would still *be* a secret."

"What do you mean?" Tori asked from across the fire ring.

"*Think* about it." Chelsea tapped her temple with her pointer finger. "How can anyone know that any of this happened? The guy it originally happened to was never heard from or seen again."

"Oh. Hmm. Girl's got a point," Gaby said. "Can't deny that logic."

"They held a séance at Camp Lakeview," Tori said mysteriously. "Randy communicated to them from beyond the grave."

"Extremely bogus," Chelsea insisted.

"Oh, you are such a downer!" Jenna said, turning around to face her. "Chelsea, can't you just play along? You always have to argue, and you don't ever help the bunk do stuff like make dinner. You can't even just wear pyjamas like the rest of us and have a good time."

As Jenna watched, something shifted in Chelsea's expression. First her eyes widened, then they narrowed, and she clenched her teeth together.

"I was *going* to put on my pyjamas, when I intruded upon Miss Thing shooting up like a drug addict."

Everyone gasped. Alex's mouth dropped open.

Chelsea blinked hard, and then her mouth set into a sharp line.

126

"Oh, you are unbelievable!" Jenna said.

"Girls? What's going on?" Belle called from her place over by the tents. She and Clarissa quickly headed for the fire ring.

Chelsea got to her feet and pushed Jenna out of her way.

"Hey!" Jenna protested.

Chelsea kept going. She was limping, as if Jenna had really hurt her. But she was totally exaggerating. Jenna hadn't stepped on her *that* hard.

"Chelsea?" Belle demanded. "Where are you going?"

"To the bathroom!"

"Take a flashlight and a buddy!" Belle called after her.

But Chelsea put on a burst of speed and disappeared into the pine trees.

"Let her go!" Jenna hissed after her. "We'll be a lot better off if Cropsy finds her!"

Tears streamed down Chelsea's face as she left the campsite. She didn't want them to hear her crying, so she started to run. She was losing it. Why did things like this happen? Was she really such an awful person? How *could* she have said something so mean about Alex?

She sobbed harder, and ran further. The moon

followed her, but she outran it and plunged into darkness. Mosquitoes descended on her; weeping, she slapped at them, whirling in a little circle.

I don't care if they send me home, she thought. *I don't care any more!*

Stars winked down watery light; she started running again, faster, harder. Her sneaker came down wrong and she zoomed down a slope, flinging out her arms to try to stay upright. Then she fell hard and kept going, skidding on her bottom. A low-lying pine branch caught her across the ankle, throwing her sideways. Her ankle twisted and she grunted, trying to grab onto something as she rolled over hard ground, rocks and pine branches.

She slid onto something rough and level. It felt like a wooden plank.

With a loud crack, it split down the middle beneath her weight. Then it gave way beneath her, and Chelsea began to fall again — straight down, dirt and wood pelting her — into the darkness.

CHAPTER SEVEN

The fire flickered on Belle's pale face as she put her hands on her hips.

"Okay, what just happened?"

Alex was crying, and Natalie and Brynn had their arms around her.

Natalie looked up. "Chelsea called Alex a drug addict," she said in a scratchy voice.

"*What?*" Belle was obviously shocked.

"I guess she thought I was taking my insulin," Alex managed, wiping her eyes with a paper napkin. "I was just doing a finger stick to check my blood sugar level."

Belle processed that. "Is that what you girls heard too?"

She looked around at the cluster of campers, and her gaze landed on Candace. Candace was already upset. She had confided in Jenna about still being afraid of the lions Jordan had told them about at the cookout, even though Jordan had said he made it up, and Jenna had obviously told other people, and now they were all laughing at her. It hurt more than she could begin to say.

Now everyone was looking at her.

I don't want to be in the middle of this, Candace thought. She didn't like being the centre of attention, ever. She was a quiet, shy person, and all the...strong personalities of the other girls in the bunk often made her feel like she was a little paper boat on a pond. She had actually started a letter to her parents before the bugle call this morning, asking them to come get her.

"Candace?" Belle prompted. "Please answer me."

Candace was torn. She knew that what Chelsea had said was horrible, but Chelsea had been trying to be nice to her earlier in the day. She wanted to say something that would smooth everything over – make Alex stop crying and get Chelsea out of trouble. But she didn't have the faintest idea where to start.

"It happened the way Nat told you," Jenna said. It hurt to talk. "It's what she said."

Everyone spoke at once, the way they usually did. Back home, Candace hung out with other low-key people, like her. Their friends took turns speaking. They were very polite. And her family was that way, too.

"I'm going after Chelsea. Everyone wait here." Belle

picked up her big flashlight from where Tori had set it down on the fire ring. Then she fished in her pocket and pulled out her cellphone, flicking it open as if she were checking something on it. Candace didn't realize that she had one with her.

"Stay put." She put the cellphone back in her pocket. "I'll be right back. And then we're going to have a full-bunk discussion about what exactly our goal is on this overnight."

Everyone looked freaked.

As Belle turned to go, Candace totally amazed herself by half-raising her hand.

"Do you want me to go with you?"

"No. Stay with Clarissa," she told Candace, gesturing at their CIT, who nodded.

"Everyone will," Clarissa assured her.

Belle flicked on her flashlight, and then she stomped off into the trees.

"So much for our great bonding experience," Gaby groused. She looked at Clarissa. "We're going to be booted, huh?"

"Oh, I'm not so sure about that," Clarissa said. She sounded completely unconvincing. "But we're not off to a real great start."

"It's Chelsea who should be booted," Valerie whispered hotly.

"Yeah," Brynn chimed in. "What a horrible thing to say to Alex."

"She didn't even help with dinner or anything," Valerie added.

"She...she tried to," Candace pointed out. Her cheeks were hot and the back of her neck tingled. Valerie intimidated her. They all intimidated her. The only Camp Lakeview bunkmate she had been completely comfortable around was Karen, and she hadn't come back this summer.

I wish I hadn't, either.

"What do you mean?" Clarissa asked her.

"She tried to," Candace said again. "She tried to gather firewood, and she tried to help build the fire, and she tried to grill the hamburgers." She moved her shoulders. "But everyone else kept telling her they'd do it, like the way she was doing it wasn't good enough."

"That doesn't erase what she said to Alex," Natalie whispered.

"Candace, what exactly did she say?" Clarissa asked her.

Now Candace knew she was really in the spotlight. She felt like she was onstage all by herself, with no clothes on.

She cleared her throat. "She said that she went back

to her tent to change, but 'Miss Thing was shooting up like a drug addict'. Alex has to take insulin because she's a diabetic," Candace blurted, then flooded with humiliation because of course Clarissa knew that. She was just so *nervous*. "No offence, Alex."

"So she didn't exactly say that Alex *is* a drug addict," Clarissa commented.

Alex wiped her eyes. "No, she didn't," she said. "I don't know why I started crying. I mean, everyone in the bunk knows I have to take insulin. I'm just really emotional. I'm not sure why."

"It was a mean thing to say," Brynn insisted loyally. "I would have cried too."

"Alex and Chelsea aren't even in the same tent," Natalie said. "Chelsea said she was going to change into her pyjamas, but she didn't. She just wanted to spy on Alex."

"That doesn't sound too likely, does it?" Clarissa asked gently.

"It does if this is your third summer with Chelsea," Jenna retorted.

"Oh, *nice*. Remember that part about the Camp Lakeview family spirit?" Gaby croaked angrily. "You people sure don't have it." She turned to Clarissa. "Chelsea and I didn't mention it before, Clarissa, but all these *nice* girls said some really mean things about

Chelsea and me when they found out we were going to be in the same bunk with them. When she overheard them, she cried all the way to the bunk."

Everyone got quiet. "It's true. I did say something really awful," Natalie admitted. Natalie looked over at Gaby. "I didn't know Chelsea told you, Gaby. I'm so sorry."

"Me too," Jenna added in a low voice. She took a deep breath. "I was nasty."

"And me," Alex murmured. "I was there too."

"Well, it sounds like we have a lot of talking to do after Belle comes back," Clarissa said. "I'm very disappointed in you girls. No wonder Chelsea's upset. On top of worrying about her father...you *do* know he's sick, right?"

Natalie winced and nodded. So did Jenna.

"Of all of us, I should have been more understanding," Alex said.

"Well, you weren't," Gaby flung at her. "If I were Chelsea, I'd take off and I'd never come back here. I didn't want to come back this year, either, but my mom wanted me to try one more summer."

"Maybe this is what Dr. Steve was talking about," Alyssa suggested. "All this stuff *we* haven't been talking about."

That was pure Alyssa, Candace thought. She didn't

talk much, but when she said something, it was worth waiting for.

"Maybe so," Clarissa said.

"Also?" Jenna began. "Candace, I am really sorry I made that crack about the lions." Her cheeks turned pink.

"It's okay," Candace murmured. But it wasn't. She was humiliated.

After that, the conversation died. Candace figured the bunk was waiting for Belle to come back with Chelsea. She wondered what would happen then. She didn't know if things were going to get worse or better for their bunk.

The propane lantern made a funny sputtering sound that caught Candace off guard. She thought about getting *The Lord of the Rings* out of her backpack. She was halfway through the second book. But she didn't move to do it. Everyone stayed as they were, in a kind of holding pattern.

Clarissa went to her tent and got the scavenger hunt clipboard, then sat down at the picnic table and began to work by the light of the lantern. It sputtered again. She started fiddling with the handle. The others began to talk to one another in twos and threes.

Jenna told Candace again that she was sorry, and went off to talk to Natalie, Tori and Brynn.

Alex sat down beside Candace. "Is that true? Did Chelsea try to help make dinner like that? Because I didn't even notice."

Candace hesitated. Then she said, "You kind of got on her case when she dropped the ketchup bottle on your tomatoes."

"Maybe she was trying to make more ketchup," Alex said, obviously trying to make a little joke. Candace didn't know what to say.

"It was brave of you to stick up for Chelsea," Alex went on.

"Thanks." She appreciated the compliment, but she still felt self-conscious.

After a while, Alex got up and talked to Brynn, Priya and Jenna. They came over and told Candace that they hadn't been laughing at her. They went on and on about it, just like Jenna had, and she really wished they would just let it go.

"Don't you think they should be back by now?" Alex asked, mercifully changing the subject. She looked off in the direction Chelsea and Belle had both gone.

"Maybe something's wrong," Natalie piped up, straining her voice. She looked expectantly at Clarissa.

"Let's give them a little more time before we interrupt them," Clarissa said.

A few more minutes passed. The fire snapped and popped, sending sparks into the sky...

...the sky that seemed a little...cloudy. It was harder to see the stars. And the glow of the big, white moon was blurry and indistinct.

Candace frowned. Then she craned her neck and gazed beyond the campfire, between the trees, at Shadow Lake.

A thin layer of fog was rising off the water.

"You guys?" she said softly. "Look at that."

She pointed to the fog. Everyone stood as Clarissa picked up the lantern and walked towards the boulders, staring at the lake.

"It's just like in Tori's story about Cropsy," Brynn said.

"It's just fog," Gaby snapped. But her voice wobbled a little.

"Hmm, if that fog rolls in, we may have some problems navigating," Clarissa muttered.

Then the lantern flickered and went out. Candace caught her breath. Except for the firelight, the campsite fell into darkness. The glow of the flames danced on the girls' faces as they watched Clarissa turning the knob.

Clarissa pulled a small pocket flashlight out of her shorts and turned it on. It was much fainter than Belle's killer flashlight, but at least it was something.

"Can you see the matches, Valerie?" she asked. "I think they're on the table."

"Sure thing," Valerie said.

Valerie bumped into a few of the girls as she made her way to the table. After some groping, she found the box and brought it back to Clarissa.

While Valerie aimed the flashlight, Clarissa set the lantern on the edge of the fire ring, took the glass bowl off the lantern's base, got a match out of the box, and tried to light the wick.

Nothing happened.

"No way," Clarissa said in disgust. "I think we're out of propane."

"Great," Gaby said.

"It's getting foggier," Brynn announced.

Candace checked. Sure enough, the fog on the surface was thicker. It was swirling around like it was boiling, and beginning to rise like steam.

"This is creeping me out a little," Brynn confessed.

"Me too," Candace murmured.

The lantern flared back on. Everyone cheered.

"I don't think there's much left." Clarissa carried the lantern back to the table and set it down. Her flashlight beam was a welcome circle of light, even if it was pretty weak.

"Chelsea might come back if I apologize to her in

private," Natalie ventured. "That's what I should have done in the first place."

"Nat's right," Jenna said. "I should too." All Candace could see was her profile, thrown against the campfire.

An owl hooted. Another answered it. Candace looked up at the tall pines and swallowed hard. She knew it was stupid to be afraid of lions, but what about other wild animals? Were there bears in the woods?

Clarissa thought for a moment. "All right. I'm going to see what's going on."

"Please, let me go with you," Natalie said.

"Me too," Jenna said. "We *need* to apologize."

Clarissa paused. "Okay. You two come with me. Everyone else, you're under strict orders *not to move*. Do you understand? Stay here. We'll be right back."

Candace nodded like a bobblehead. She *definitely* planned not to move.

Clarissa pointed her flashlight in the direction Chelsea and Belle had gone. "Okay, Natalie, Jenna, let's go."

Then the three left the campsite.

That left seven other girls besides Candace: Gaby, Priya, Tori, Valerie, Alex, Alyssa and Brynn.

"Should I break out some magazines?" Valerie asked.

"Nat brought a ton of them. We could see if we can find articles about other campouts that have fallen apart, and how they got put back together again."

Candace wondered if Valerie was trying to make a joke. It didn't seem very funny. She stared at the fog and chewed on her thumbnail. It was a bad habit, but she was very nervous at the moment and she couldn't stop herself.

"Pass," Priya said. "Does anyone want another s'more?"

"Pass." Tori groaned. "I have eaten way too many carbs lately." She counted them off. "Hamburger bun, s'more, French toast, more s'mores..."

Candace squinted at the fog as it cloaked the surface of the lake. Was that a dark blotch in the middle of it? A *boat*-shaped dark blotch?

"You guys?" She got up and craned her neck. "Do you see anything strange out there?"

"Like what?" Priya stood and walked boldly towards the slope that looked down over the water. Candace wanted to tell her to stay back, but she didn't want anyone to make fun of her again.

Except for Candace, the others rose and followed after Priya.

"It's just fog," Gaby said after a beat. "So? No big deal."

"It's thick spooky-ooky fog," Alex remarked.

They were quiet for a moment as they spread out across the top of the embankment. In the fire ring, a piece of burning wood popped and snapped.

"Hey, I *do* see it," Priya announced. "What do you think it is?"

"Cropsy's boat, mwahaha." Valerie made her hands into claws. "Sorry, just one." She slipped her right arm around her body, holding up her left "claw".

"He didn't have a boat," Gaby said, sounding irritated. "Randy had a boat."

"Eww, we were swimming in dead-guy water! With a cut-off arm in it!" Brynn cried.

"That was just a *story*." Gaby huffed. "And besides, everything would have decomposed a long, long time ago."

"Eww, eww, eww!" Brynn cried. She tapped her feet on the ground as if she were trying to shake off all traces of supreme grossness.

"It doesn't look like a boat to me." Alex tilted her head and looked this way and that. "It looks like a rock."

"Are there any rocks in Shadow Lake? Big rocks like that?" Valerie pointed at the shape. "I don't remember any big rocks."

"I don't care. I'm going to have nightmares all night!

I'm going back to the campfire," Brynn announced. She came over to Candace and sat down.

"Someone should write a play about this," she told Candace. "It's scarier than *The Legend of Sleepy Hollow*."

Candace wondered why that was a good thing.

"It's hardly original. There've only been about two hundred horror movies just like this," Gaby sniped.

Priya, Alex and Alyssa left their vantage posts and came back to the campfire, too.

"It's okay," Priya whispered to Candace. "They'll be back soon."

Tori, Valerie and Gaby stayed on the embankment, watching the fog, staring at the boatlike shadow on Shadow Lake.

Trust our bunk to have an overnight like this, Gaby thought.

She was so tired of all the drama. And the freakiness, with the fog moving in off the lake, and the strange shape in the lake that really *did* look like a boat, and the logs in the fire popping...

...and something creeping just off to the right, rustling through the bushes...

She quickly turned her head and squinted in the direction of the rustling.

"What is it?" Tori asked her.

142

"Chelse?" Gaby called. Her voice was hoarse, just like everyone else's. They were all croaking from the campfire singing. "Is that you?"

There was no answer.

The noise grew lower...and a little closer.

"Do you hear that?" Gaby asked.

"It's probably just a little animal, like a possum," Valerie said. "Or a bird."

"It sounds like footsteps," Gaby insisted.

"It does not. It sounds like an animal," Valerie argued, but the quaver in her voice betrayed her uncertainty. Then she raised her voice and rasped, "Chelsea? Belle? Clarissa?"

The creeping noise stopped.

"There. You heard *that*, right?" Gaby said.

"Hello?" Valerie called, her voice scratchy and shrill. "Anyone there?"

Nothing.

Gaby rubbed her arms, even though she wasn't cold.

"How long have they all been gone?" she asked. "Someone should have been back by now. I mean, even if Chelsea is having a major meltdown, they'd send someone back to tell the rest of us that they haven't, like, *died* or something."

"They haven't died," Valerie snorted. "They're probably just calming Chelsea down."

143

"Maybe Jenna went psycho again," Gaby said. "Like she did in the bunk. You know, not everything is always Chelsea's fault."

"Hey, we all went a little psycho," Tori reminded her. Then she sighed. "You know, guys, maybe Dr. Steve called it right. We're the bunk from hell."

"We are not. We're just...cranky," Brynn said. "Hormonally challenged. My mother says all girls go off the deep end when they hit their teens. We are almost there, girlfriends."

No one spoke for a moment.

Tori cupped her hands around her mouth and faced the thick, dark woods. "Chelsea! We're sorry! Come back!" Her voice barely registered above a whisper.

They all screeched, hoarsely shouting all the names of the missing.

"Belle!"

"Clarissa!"

"Nat! Jenna! Chelsea!"

As before, there was no answer, only the lonely hoot of an owl.

After half a minute or so, Tori gestured at the lake. "Guys, the fog is getting thicker. And it's started to creep up the bank."

"It's like that movie called *The Fog*," Priya said. "All

these dead guys are inside the fog and when it swirls up around you, they get you!"

"Oh," Candace fretted.

"Did you guys see that Johnny Depp pirate movie? When the moonlight shines on the pirates, and they look like skeletons?" Valerie mock shuddered. "Brrr!"

"Let's talk about something else," Alex suggested. "Like the social. What do you think the theme will be this year?"

"Pirates of the Caribbean," Valerie said, snickering a little.

Gaby thought of how pale Belle must look out there in the forest and had a crazy micro-moment where she thought, *What if Belle really is a vampire?* But she knew she was just thinking like that to scare herself.

Right?

"Guys?" Tori croaked again.

The fog was creeping over her, Gaby's and Valerie's ankles. Gaby took a step back.

It wafted forward, almost like it was getting ready to pounce.

"Eek! Spooky fog!" Valerie whisper-cried. She turned on her heel and ran back to the campfire. Tori followed after her.

"It's just fog," Gaby said, but she ran away from it too.

CHAPTER EIGHT

Gaby felt a little guilty looking through Clarissa and Belle's tent for more flashlights, but they still hadn't returned, and the fog had crept up from the lake to encircle the fire ring. She wondered if the fog had moved even deeper into the forest further down the shore. That would explain why Belle and the others hadn't come back — because they couldn't see which way they were going. Maybe they had gotten so far away, they couldn't hear everyone yelling for them. Not that they were yelling very loudly.

"Are you thinking what I'm thinking?" Valerie asked her as she pulled a tube of lipgloss from Clarissa's daypack, unscrewed the wand, and pulled the lantern closer to check out the colour. Then, as if she felt guilty too, she hastily reinserted the wand and put the lipgloss back in the pack.

The gas hiss was freaky, like the lantern was breathing.

Gaby was afraid that might mean it was finally running out of propane. They had to find some flashlights, and quick.

"I don't know," Gaby said. "What are you thinking?"

"That this could be some kind of prank they're pulling to get us to 'bond'?" Valerie made air quotes.

"You watch too much reality TV," Gaby replied.

"I'm serious. Think about it." Valerie returned to her search. "Ooh, Clarissa has that new eyeshadow I've been wanting." She held it up.

"Valerie, we're not doing makeovers. Just look for flashlights," Gaby snapped at her.

"Hey, you're not the boss of me," Valerie snapped back.

Gaby flared. She didn't like being here, didn't like looking through their counsellors' private belongings, didn't like anything about this campout. She couldn't stop herself from saying, "I thought you were so great at getting along with other people."

"I am," Valerie insisted. "*Usually.*"

"What are you saying? That I'm hard to deal with?" Gaby said, as she moved from Belle's duffel bag to another corner of the tent. She made out the shape of a box and pulled it open. Taking a breath, she reached her hand inside. She felt cold metal and wrapped her hand around it.

"Flashlights," she announced, pulling one out. She flicked on the light, not realizing she was aiming it directly at Valerie, who raised her hand in protest.

"Hey!" Valerie said.

"Sorry." Gaby shined the flashlight into the box. "There's probably half a dozen of them in here." She moved them around until she could see the bottom of the box. The milky light bathing the flashlights reminded her of sunken treasure. "But no cellphone."

"Hey, here are the treasure hunt notes," Valerie announced, picking up the familiar-looking clipboard.

"Let me see them." Gaby eagerly held out her hand.

Valerie demurred, leaving the clipboard in her lap. "Belle doesn't want us to see them."

Gaby huffed. "Maybe there's a clue about where everybody has disappeared to."

"They haven't disappeared," Valerie insisted. "We just don't know where they are." Valerie reached out and took a flashlight, then flicked it on and focused it under her chin. "I suggest that aliens abducted them, mwahaha."

"That's not funny."

Valerie put the clipboard beside the opening to the tent. "I'll tell you what. If they're not back in a few minutes, we'll look at the notes, okay?"

"Whatever," Gaby said. "Let's keep looking." She added, "Maybe we can find the SPF 5000 sunscreen Belle uses to stay so pale."

That got a chuckle out of Valerie.

Then Gaby said, more seriously, "I've been thinking. Maybe she was really sick and she's been in a hospital. You know how she can be kind of edgy? Maybe she just got out and she's not used to being back in the outside world."

"Maybe she's been in a *mental* hospital," Valerie said. "Maybe she took an axe with her into the woods and she's killed them all!" She slapped her cheeks. "Oh no! She's Cropsy's daughter!"

"*Why* do you keep doing that?" Gaby half-shouted at her. "Aren't things scary enough for you?"

"It just comes naturally," Valerie admitted. "My head just goes there."

That felt like an apology. Gaby calmed down and nodded as she flicked another flashlight on and off. She was testing them.

"Maybe you should go back to Hollywood with Tori and become a movie director," Gaby said.

"LaToya and I are talking about going to a performing arts high school," Valerie told her.

"I'll bet that's a big hit with your parents," Gaby replied. "Mine are always pouring on the pressure.

'Get good grades. Go to a good college.'"

"Actually, my stepmother's very supportive," Valerie said. "But it is making my dad a little crazy."

"My parents are both attorneys," Gaby said. "They work all the time. They've already told me that I should go to law school, and I'm thinking, 'Why? So I can work all the time, too?'"

"Wow. That *is* pressure." Valerie dropped her hands onto her knees. "Well, I think we can safely say that there are no cellphones in here."

Gaby ran her flashlight along the floor of the tent, then up one side and along the ceiling. As she moved down the other side, something flickered in her side vision and she jerked her flashlight back.

"Hey, did you just see something?" she asked Valerie.

"Something like what?"

"I don't know. I thought I saw something." Gaby moved her flashlight slowly.

"Stop it. I'm not falling for it."

"I'm serious," Gaby insisted. "I—"

"Something's coming!" Valerie hissed.

Footsteps padded towards the tent. Both girls aimed their flashlights at the opening.

It was Tori.

"You scared us half to death!" Gaby cried.

"Sorry," Tori said. She ducked her head in. "Did you find anything?"

"Flashlights," Gaby proclaimed. "And the notes for the scavenger hunt." She held them up them to show Tori.

"No man may look upon them and live," Valerie said.

"Lucky thing none of us are men," Tori drawled.

"If they don't come back soon, I say we look at the notes," Gaby told Tori. "Valerie's got this theory that all this is part of the bonding experience," she said as she crawled on her hands and knees from the back of the tent.

Tori snorted. "I've got this theory that we have stumbled into a bad horror movie."

"Great minds think alike," Valerie said and edged her way out of the door, flashlight and clipboard in hand.

Gaby said, "Well, I don't like watching horror movies, and I like being in them even less."

"Maybe we *should* look at the scavenger hunt notes," Tori said. "What if they left us a note, like, *Dear Bunk Psycho, welcome to* Survivor, *Camp Lakeview-style. While we are gone, your job is to build a hut and search for edible berries and not snark one another to death. It's a whole big bonding thing.*"

"We have tents and lots of food," Gaby pointed

out, ignoring Tori's snarking comment. "But you might be right. I say let's check the notes."

"Okay, I'm outvoted," Valerie announced. "We'll check."

The trio returned to the campfire. The other girls were sitting at the two picnic tables, most with their knees tucked under their chins as if they were trying to avoid the fog that rolled along the ground like waves. Someone had added a bunch of wood to the campfire and the flames flickered over their tired, anxious faces.

"We found flashlights," Gaby said cheerfully. She gestured to the box Tori was carrying.

"But no cellphone?" Candace asked.

"No," Gaby admitted. "But we know Belle has one. Maybe she's calling for help right now."

"Which implies that we *need* help," Priya said.

The group fell silent for a moment. Gaby didn't know what to say to that.

Candace looked up at her. "Do *you* think we need help, Gaby?"

The bunk waited for Gaby's answer. Somehow she had become a leader. That seemed to happen to her a lot. She'd say or do something and the next thing she knew, other people were either doing what she asked, or getting mad at her for asking them to do it in the first place.

"I don't know, but we have the scavenger hunt notes, and we're going to look at them and see if this is part of the game. Okay?"

"Good idea." Alex gave her head a decisive nod. She looked at the others. One by one, they nodded too. Wow, everyone agreed on something.

"I hope we don't get in trouble," Candace said.

"They're the ones in trouble," Brynn said in her hoarse, scratchy voice, "for leaving us alone."

"You have a point. Let's see what's going on." Gaby reached for the clipboard. Valerie handed it to her.

"One," Gaby read. *"Divide the girls up into groups. Two, we hide! We (along with the bags and bags of penny candy we'll be holding) are the prizes of the scavenger hunt!"*

Stunned murmurs went around the group as they took that in.

"No way! This *is* a prank! I'm going to kill them both!" Brynn pantomimed choking someone.

"Me too," Tori agreed.

"Wait a minute," Alex said. "That doesn't follow. *Chelsea* was the reason Belle left. And Clarissa went after Belle."

"Chelsea was in on it. Remember when Chelsea left us at the lake? That's when they must have planned the whole thing," Brynn said, her voice filled with awe. "So then Chelsea pretended to be a total brat and

153

march off so Belle could split, and then Clarissa could split. Wow, Chelsea deserves an Academy Award for her performance. I bought it."

"No way. Chelsea would *not* say something mean about Alex for the sake of a stupid game," Alyssa insisted.

"I totally agree with you." Gaby was pleased to hear someone stick up for Chelsea. Sure, sometimes the girl was irritating, but wasn't everybody?

Brynn shrugged. "So maybe Belle found Chelsea after she stomped off and told her to play along. And then Clarissa realized Belle had taken advantage of the situation and started the scavenger hunt. So *she* left."

"But she took Natalie and Jenna with her," Alex argued.

"Besides, we were going to do the scavenger hunt tomorrow. In the daylight," Priya put in. She looked at the other girls. "Right? Isn't that what Belle told us?"

"I...think so," Tori said. She tilted her head. "I can't remember. But maybe that was to throw us off. Maybe taking Natalie and Jen was to confuse us too."

"Guys, please. Think." Alex picked up the clipboard and scanned it, turning the first page and running her finger down the next page. "There is *no way* that a camp counsellor would leave us alone and then expect us to look for her in the woods. That's totally against all the Camp Lakeview rules."

"No *normal* camp counsellor," Valerie shot back. "We've already established that Belle is a little bit...unusual."

"Weird," Brynn said.

"Spooky," Tori agreed.

"Wacko," Valerie added.

"Not *that* wacko," Gaby insisted.

Brynn folded her arms across her chest. "If it's not a game, why haven't they come back?"

"Because they're lost?" Alex suggested.

"In that case...Chelsea!" Brynn tried to yell, but her voice completely gave out. "Belle! You guys!" she whispered.

Everyone joined in again. As before, there was no answer to their lame distress calls.

Gaby gazed at Alex. "What else is in the notes?"

"They were going to make trails for us through the woods," Alex replied. "Bend back branches and tie pieces of cloth around tree trunks. It says to follow the map."

Alex flipped through the pages to the end. "Maybe this is supposed to be a map, but I don't know how to read it."

She showed it to Gaby. It was a big oval with a bunch of little drawings and X's on it.

"I think this is a big loop around the lake," Gaby said.

"That can't be right," Alex argued. "They wouldn't make a scavenger hunt around the entire lake. It's huge."

"This part looks like our campsite," Gaby said, pointing to a tiny upside-down V shape. And look, if you go from the campsite, there's an X that should be..." She looked to the left. "...exactly where Chelsea and everyone else took off."

Tori leaned over her shoulder. "You're right."

"I'm going to go see if I can find them." Picking up the clipboard, Gaby got to her feet.

"Gaby, no." Priya frowned. "Clarissa told us to stay here."

"And every time someone leaves, they don't come back," Candace added in a soft, frightened voice.

"Well, *I'm* going. Enough's enough." Gaby took a flashlight out of the box and flicked it on.

"You can't go alone," Tori announced. She flashed Gaby a half-smile and got a flashlight, too. She flicked it on and ran the beam around the outskirts of the campfire.

"Me three," Valerie said.

Gaby looked at Valerie and Tori, surprised that both of them had volunteered to go with her. She thought they didn't like her.

"Don't, you guys," Alyssa insisted. "We're probably wrong. I'm sure they really went to get Chelsea and then they got turned around in the fog. They'll be back as soon as it clears up."

"And they'll find out we've ruined the scavenger hunt," Candace said.

Gaby tried to sound light-hearted as she said, "Well, *we'll* find out soon enough. Coming, ladies?"

As Tori, Valerie and Gaby left the campsite, Tori wondered if she had just made a big mistake. In every scary movie she had ever watched, this was exactly what the characters did – split up – and then the crazed slasher-guy picked them off. She didn't know why on earth she had volunteered to go. She just...had. She had to do something. She couldn't stand just sitting there, wondering what was going on.

But that's what the characters in the slasher movies do, and we always crack up and say they deserve what they get, because they're so stupid, she thought.

"Chelsea?" Gaby rasped as they walked into the dense woods. "Belle?"

And then the slasher-guy starts following them through the woods. They're easy to track, because they make so much noise.

"Chelsea, we're sorry!" Valerie whispered. "Oh,

157

why did we sing so much? I can barely talk!"

Above them, broad-leafed trees and pines rose like enormous gargoyles. The long branches bobbed and shifted like leathery wings. The hot, moist air hung thickly around Tori like a net. She slapped her arm, heard a buzzing in her ear, and shooed a mosquito away.

As they walked, the three bunkmates aimed their flashlights downwards, but the beams bounced off the thick fog. The mist had risen to the tops of Tori's knees. She walked carefully, feeling rocks and tree roots underneath her sneaker soles; but she still tripped over something strange and hard — *tree root, branch,* she told herself — and she jerked when something skittered from beneath it through the fog, hidden from her scrutiny.

This is such a horrible idea, she thought again, as her heart pounded.

"Hey, look at this," Valerie said.

She shone her flashlight on the bent-back branches of a spindly bush.

"No. Way," Gaby said excitedly. She looked down at the map. "They must have made this path."

"When?" Tori asked, examining the broken branches. "They never left the campsite."

"Sure they did," Gaby insisted. "Belle was with us at the lake. She made sure all of us were there. Remember how she kept counting us? She got upset when she realized Chelsea was missing."

"She got upset because she's our counsellor," Tori said. "She's supposed to know where we are at all times."

"*And* because maybe Clarissa snuck off then and started making the trails for the hunt while we were in the lake," Valerie said, clearly following Gaby's lead. "Maybe that's why Belle wanted us to go swimming in the first place."

"Oh. That works." Tori felt twenty times better. Make that a hundred. She hadn't even realized how nervous she'd been until now, when her knees went a little wobbly with relief.

"Okay, if we're right, there should be more of these little markers," Valerie said. "So hopefully, they're not too far apart and we can find the next one."

The three moved forward, each girl stepping cautiously through the fog. Now that it didn't seem as threatening, the thick blanket of white reminded Tori of the powdery snow in Tahoe. She imagined trying to snowboard on top of the fog and smiled to herself.

"Yesss!" Gaby shone her flashlight on another broken branch. "We're hot on the trail." She cleared her throat and called out, "Chelsea! We know you're out here!"

"Chelsea!" Tori squeaked. "Belle!"

They stood still, listening.

"No one can hear us. We're too hoarse," Gaby said.

Including everybody back at the campsite, Tori thought. *In the woods, no one can hear you scream. If you can scream.*

They walked on, shining their flashlights over tree limbs and branches. There were no more bent-back stubs.

They came to a low-hanging pine bough that stopped Gaby in her tracks.

"Hmm," Gaby said, shining her flashlight on the map. "Maybe we should turn."

"Left or right?" Valerie moved the beam of her flashlight over the dense stands of trees. "It said they would tie pieces of cloth around tree trunks. Do you see any cloth?"

They turned around in a little circle as the fog billowed and churned around their hips. There were no pieces of cloth. There were no broken branches.

We were wrong, Tori thought. Her mouth went dry. Fear danced up her spine.

"I kind of think we should go back," she said. "Maybe a wild animal broke those other branches."

"It looked like someone did it on purpose," Gaby argued.

"It did," Valerie agreed.

"Maybe only because that was what we were hoping

160

to see," Tori insisted. "We're going to get lost. We should go back."

"Two more minutes," Gaby said, tapping the map. "And if we don't find another set of broken branches, we'll turn around."

Tori wanted to say no. She wanted to go back *now*. They didn't even have a watch to figure out when two minutes had passed. She thought about all the lectures she'd had in school and at home about giving in to peer pressure. She didn't smoke, didn't drink, and had kissed her boyfriend exactly twice. Tromping through the woods like this was a bad idea and she knew it. But it was hard to say no to Gaby and Valerie.

"Two minutes," Gaby said again.

"Come on, Tori," Valerie urged. "Maybe Chelsea got hurt and they can't leave her, and they need our help."

Then they would be calling out for help. She thought about that. Why hadn't they heard Belle or Clarissa yelling? Maybe they *were* hiding. Maybe this really was the scavenger hunt.

Tori sighed. "I'll give you a minute and a half."

"You're on." Gaby grinned at her. "We'll turn back in ninety seconds."

"One Mississippi," Tori intoned.

"Let's go to the right," Gaby said.

They walked a few metres to the right, Gaby first.

Valerie was just a little way behind her, and Tori fell back a little when she skirted around a fallen tree trunk.

Without warning, the ground angled sharply downward, and it was covered with a blanket of dried pine needles and crinkly leaves that made it as slippery as a water slide. As Gaby's sneakers began to scoot out from underneath her, Valerie caught her forearm. Then she, too, lost her balance – and the two fell onto their butts. They started zooming down the incline.

"Help!" Gaby whisper-cried.

They disappeared inside a thick bank of fog. Tori could still hear them sliding, but she couldn't see them at all. She took a step forward, peering hard...

"Whoa!" Tori croaked, as she started to fall too. She reached overhead for a pine branch, but she wasn't fast enough. She landed hard on her bottom and sailed into the roiling mist after her two friends.

"Guys! Guys!" she whispered. "Look out below!"

Instinctively she rolled to the side to slow her descent, but then the ground dropped away beneath her shoulder and she sailed into thin air – or rather, thick fog. She reached out her hands, trying to grab at a branch, anything to catch herself – and thumped even harder on a patch of ground.

Her way made slick by pine needles, she kept sliding through the fog, then finally skidded to a stop.

"Tori! Are you okay?" Gaby whispered from somewhere above her.

Tori rolled over on her back. Fog surrounded her, and when she raised her hand in front of herself, she could barely see it. Looking past her hand, she could just make out Gaby's silhouette in the fog. Gaby was standing about five metres above Tori on an outcropping of rock.

"Ow," Tori replied. She sat up and tested herself for broken bones. Everything appeared to be working. "I guess I'm okay."

Then she heard someone moving directly behind her. It had to be Valerie. It was lucky they hadn't collided.

She turned around. The fog was too thick for her to see Valerie, but she heard her shuffling through the pine needles. She was panting heavily.

"Tori? I can't see you any more," Gaby said. "Valerie, can you see her?"

Valerie?

"No," Valerie replied...from the same place as Gaby.

Tori gazed up to see the dim outline of Valerie beside Gaby on the outcropping.

But if Valerie's up there, that means...

"Chelsea? Jenna? Are you pranking us?" Tori asked fearfully as she scooted backwards on her butt. She cleared her throat. "Gaby? Can you see me now?"

"No," Gaby said.

"I think...we're not alone," Tori said.

"What?" Gaby said.

"Guys? Listen," Tori urged them.

But there was nothing but silence. The shuffling and panting had stopped.

Tori swallowed hard. "Chelsea?" she said. "Is that you? Everything's okay. Everyone is worried about you. No one is going to yell at you or send you home. Let's go back to camp now."

The panting started again.

Then something poked her shoulder.

She screamed, but it came out as a strangled squeak. She turned around, grabbing bushes, roots, dragging herself up the slope, crying and grunting.

"Help! Help!" she whispered.

"Tori? What's wrong? What's happening?" Gaby honked.

Tori fought her way up the incline, through thick, rolling fog, to feel her hand batting someone else's hand. Strong fingers closed around her.

"It's me, Valerie. I've got you. Gaby, help me pull her up!"

Hand over hand, they half-pulled, half-dragged her up. Tori couldn't see either of them. She fought to catch her breath.

"Someone's down there!"

"It's a prank," Valerie said. "Belle! Clarissa!"

"I don't think it's them!" Tori grabbed Valerie's hands. "Let's get out of here!"

She started to run, and Valerie ran with her. Gaby was beside them in an instant, and they raced blindly in the fog.

A tree branch smacked Tori in the face, but she kept going, tears streaming down her cheeks. She was terrified. She kept feeling those sharp pokes against her shoulder.

Valerie stumbled. "Don't stop!" she begged.

Heavy footfalls galloped behind them. It had climbed up the slope! It was coming after them!

"It's chasing us!" Gaby said. She started to slow, as if she were going to turn around to see what it was. "Guys, is that you? Jenna? This is *not* funny!"

"Keep going!" Tori begged.

Then someone – something – started howling. It was high-pitched and angry and it followed them as they ran. It was a crazy shriek, a wild scream...

...and Tori could almost hear the words:

"Where is my arm?"

"It's Cropsy!" Tori screamed.

Squealing in terror, the three friends raced on.

CHAPTER NINE

Seated on their logs around the blazing campfire, Brynn and Priya had just scored another point off Alex, Alyssa and Candace in "Broadway Musical Singdown!" It was a version of the Colour War singdown, but tonight, nearly all the contestants were hoarse at the beginning of the competition, not the end.

The fog hung around them like heavy, wet curtains. They could barely see one another as they sat in a semicircle – Brynn at one end, Alex at the other – and they couldn't see their tents at all.

Or the lake.

Or the moon.

They had their tiny flashlights on and they were holding the singdown to keep their spirits up. It seemed too awful to admit that Tori, Valerie and Gaby had gone missing too. The first reaction of those left behind – Alex, Alyssa, Candace, Priya and Brynn – was to huddle together in frightened confusion. Then Alex had suggested they make the fire bigger and cheerier and start singing songs. The distraction had worked... at first. But now Alex, for one, was starting to feel a little jittery.

"We should do a different category, like nineties' pop hits," she said. "Brynn knows every musical ever composed!" The truth was, she didn't really care if Brynn kept winning. It was kind of funny, actually, especially because Brynn sounded like a foghorn. But Alex wanted everyone to stay interested. She knew from playing soccer that if one team started to lose all the time, it was harder for them to stay in the game. And she wanted them to stay in the game so they wouldn't get so scared they might pee their pants.

Like she was just about to do.

"It's kind of my area of expertise," Brynn semi-whispered. "Since I want to specialize in musical theatre. But if the Flame Dancers will agree that the Fireflies have won this round, I'm willing to move onto nineties' pop."

The Flame Dancers – Alex, Alyssa and Candace – looked at one another and nodded. Alyssa was nibbling on some candy and Alex wished she could have some too. Candace was biting her fingernails.

"Okay," Alex agreed. "Fireflies, you won the first

round, so you go first. Sing the first line of something nineties and we'll sing the next line."

"Let me think," Brynn said. She leaned in towards Priya. "Do you have any ideas?"

Priya and Brynn whispered together. Then Brynn made a funny, low moan deep in her chest.

"Brynn, you've got to do something that's longer than that," Alex grumped. "That's not enough of a hint."

There was a pause. "That wasn't me," Brynn said.

"Me neither," Priya said. She held up her hand. "Honest."

"Okay, then who did it?" Alex asked the group. "Is someone making some kind of a singdown dare?"

No one answered as the girls looked at one another in confusion. The seconds passed and no one confessed.

"Chelsea?" Priya ventured.

Alex waved her flashlight slowly at the perimeter of fog hanging around the campfire. She saw nothing in the dense whiteness. "Chelsea? Belle?" she called out.

There was no answer.

"Maybe it was a bullfrog," Candace suggested, hugging herself. Then she ducked her head as if she expected them to laugh at her.

"It could be a bullfrog," Alyssa said. Then a grin spread across her face. "But I'll bet it was Jenna Bloom."

Smiles grew all around. They waited a few seconds. "Okay, jig's up! The experiment was a success!" Priya said cheerily. "We've bonded! We love one another. Come on back!"

There was no answer.

"Are there bears in these woods?" Brynn asked.

"*Bears?*" Candace echoed.

"I don't think so," Alex said, but she didn't know for sure. "I don't think Dr. Steve would let us camp here if—"

She was interrupted by another low moan drifting through the fog.

Brynn jumped to her feet. "Guys? This isn't amusing!"

There was no answer. Candace whimpered. Alex put her arm around her.

"Yoo-hoo, we're done," Brynn brayed.

"*My arm,*" a voice whispered.

"Okay, now I know this is a joke!" Brynn twirled in a little circle as she shone her flashlight over the fog. "Come on out, *Cropsy!*"

"No," Candace pleaded. "Don't say his name!"

"Who's doing this?" Brynn said. "Chelsea?"

"We are not scared!" Priya squeaked.

More silence.

Nerve-racking silence.

Alex's heart hammered against her chest. Her throat was dry as a bone. She tried to tell herself that there would be a good explanation for this. Any. Second. Now.

Then suddenly, without warning, something moved in the fog. A shape jittered and shook, and Alex realized it was the branches of the broken tree beside the granite boulder. Then the bush next to it shook, hard.

"My arm!" the voice hissed.

"Eeek!" Candace cried. She bolted, grabbing her flashlight and heading in the opposite direction, towards the tents.

"Candace, no! It's a joke!" Alex managed to blurt as she raced after her. She was afraid Candace would hurt herself.

And I'm afraid, period! Alex thought. Because what if it wasn't a joke?

The fog was thin enough that she could see Candace flying a few metres ahead of her. Candace bypassed the tents and kept running, past the other granite boulder that sectioned off their camping space. Alex heard footfalls and shrill, hoarse cries as her other bunkmates rocketed after them.

They raced into unexplored territory. Fog and darkness gave way to flashes of white as the beam of Alex's flashlight danced around.

Brynn and Priya caught up with Alex and ran with her to the crest of the embankment, just as Candace and Alyssa disappeared over it.

Then a horrible wailing echoed off the sky. It sounded inhuman. Crazy. Evil.

"This is no prank!" Brynn rasped.

"Something's really after us!" Priya squealed.

The three tore down the bank. Alex half-slid, half-ran. She lost her footing, and Priya and Brynn grabbed her up, propelling her along. But she felt a sharp pain in her knee where she had landed.

"Look!" Priya cried, pointing with her flashlight.

Beneath the moonlight, close to the water's edge, two small wooden boats sat tilted on the ground. Scavenger hunt props? Or the boats of a stranger? The stranger who was chasing them?

Candace and Alyssa reached one of the boats. They gestured wildly to Alex and the others.

"Let's get in!" Candace begged. "Come on, come on!"

Brynn and Priya bolted ahead of Alex, joining Candace and Alyssa as they grouped around the back of the boat and began to push it towards the lake.

"Alex, come on!" Candace rasped, waving at her over her shoulder. "Let's get out of here!"

They reached the water's edge. Candace, Priya and

Alyssa scrabbled into the boat while Brynn held onto the stern. She looked back at Alex, who was at least five metres away. Alex's knee was aching like crazy.

"It's pulling me!" Brynn shouted. "Hurry! I can't hold it!"

Then the boat jerked out of her grasp and started moving away at a rapid clip.

"Hey! Wait!" Brynn yelled, sloshing after it.

As the girls screamed and yelled, Priya leaned over the stern, grabbed Brynn's hands, and hauled her in. Brynn tumbled into the boat.

"Hurry!" she shouted to Alex. "It's moving really fast! We don't have any oars!"

Sucking in air with each step, Alex stumbled towards them. She reached out her arms as she wobbled into the icy lake water.

"Swim, Alex!" Priya called out.

"Swim to us! Come on!" the others yelled.

Alex hesitated, staring at the cold, dark water.

Then all four of them started screaming and pointing.

"Alex! *He's behind you!*" Alyssa yelled.

Alex whirled around.

At the crest of the embankment, a tall, bulky figure stood with its legs spread wide apart, gazing down on her. The fog gathered around it was like smoke pouring off its body.

It was wearing a hockey mask and carrying a chainsaw.

And it only had one arm!

CHAPTER TEN

The powerful cascade of the waterfall sucked up the sound as Nat, Clarissa and Jenna counted to three, nodded at one another, and shouted, "Chelsea! Belle!"

Nat's voice was nearly gone. Jenna's, too. Nat was scared and she was tired and she wanted to go back to the campsite. Clarissa had confessed that she'd made a wrong turn a long time ago – actually, several – and she'd been trying ever since to get them back to the campsite.

Although Nat was trying not to show it, she was beginning to panic. The fog kept circling around the three of them, making it more and more difficult to see. The story of Cropsy had freaked her out in a fun way at the campfire, but now, lost deep in the woods with the thickening fog, it seemed less like a campfire story and more like something that could happen in real life.

As she scanned the dense forest for signs of

movement, something bumped into her from behind. She almost screamed at the top of her lungs as she whirled around.

It was Jenna.

"Whoops, sorry," she said, as Nat tried to cram her heart back into her chest.

Clarissa pulled her cellphone from the pocket of her cargo shorts. "Let me try to call Belle again." She pressed a couple of buttons.

"Or the police," Nat said.

"Them too," Clarissa agreed.

Nat crossed her fingers and waited. "Maybe it will work this time," Jenna said.

Then Clarissa sighed, and Nat knew Clarissa still had no signal.

"Maybe when we reach higher ground," Clarissa said cheerily.

"Ya-huh," Jenna said under her breath.

"For all we know, Belle found Chelsea and they're back with the bunk, devouring s'mores." Clarissa put the phone back in her pocket.

"Sounds good," Jenna said.

"Let's go this way," Clarissa suggested. Nat knew the CIT had no idea which way she was going. But she didn't know what else to do besides follow her. Her hand shook as she held back a branch for Jenna.

After Jenna went past, Nat lost her balance for a second and let go of the branch. It smacked her in the face with a sharp sting.

She almost started crying. She wished she hadn't insisted on coming with Clarissa. Why hadn't she listened when Belle had told them to stay at the campfire?

Because I felt bad about dissing Chelsea, she thought. She hadn't even given Chelsea the benefit of the doubt before deciding that having her in their bunk was going to ruin the summer. She thought about what Candace had said. Everybody *was* criticizing Chelsea's attempts to help with dinner. Clarissa was right. Who'd want to hang out with a bunch of people like Bunk 5A?

"We're going to be okay," Jenna said beside her.

"Yeah, but is Chelsea?" Natalie asked her.

Jenna sighed heavily. "You've been thinking about her too, huh? I feel so rotten. I went on like I'm all that—"

"I was right there with you," Nat interrupted her. "Even after we accidentally hurt her feelings, I was still on her at the campsite. It's like...I have 'be mean to Chelsea' on my to-do list."

"I know." Jenna groaned. "If she'd just..." She trailed off. "I mean, seriously, Nat, she *has* been hard to deal with. And I know her dad is sick and all, but it seems

176

like every time she could say something nice or something snarky, she goes for column B."

"Not always," Nat insisted. "We just wait for it. We look for it."

Jenna brought the beam of her flashlight close, and Nat saw the troubled expression on her friend's face. "I blew it with Candace, too. She was so hurt. I'm such a moron. I deserve to be hunted down like a dog and have my arm cut off by a raving lunatic."

"Jenna!" Nat swatted her forearm. "Don't say things like that. They aren't funny. Not right now, anyway."

Jenna grimaced. "More evidence. Stuff just pops out of my mouth. It's the curse of Jenna Bloom. I'll do better. I swear I will."

"We'll both do better," Nat promised.

Slightly ahead of them, Clarissa stopped. She looked up at the moon and then at the dark woods. Back up at the moon.

Back at the dark woods.

"I think we take a left here," she said.

"She has no clue," Jenna whispered to Nat. "She's totally lost."

"I know," Nat whispered back. "But what else can we do?"

"Sit down and wait for someone to find us?" Jenna suggested. She and Nat gazed at each other.

"Like Cropsy?" Nat asked under her breath.

"C'mon already – he's just made up," Jenna insisted. But she didn't sound very convincing.

Then, almost as if it had been dumped on them like a waterfall, the fog swirled around them, and Nat couldn't see a thing except for the gauzy beam from her flashlight. She tried touching her hand to her face and couldn't even see her fingers.

Her panic went into overdrive.

"Oh, man," Jenna whispered. "I'm going to lose it."

"Okay, this is just too much," Clarissa said, sounding frustrated. "Let's stop moving around, girls. Just find a place to plant yourself and sit down."

Nat felt around for something to perch on. She didn't like stretching out her hands and touching things she couldn't see, but she didn't seem to have much of a choice.

"I can't see anything," Nat protested. "I can't even see my feet."

"It'll be okay, Natalie. Just sit down," Clarissa said.

"Okay." Nat's fingertips trailed along the rough but level length of a fallen log. "I found a place. I'm sitting."

"Right beside you, Goode," Jenna said. She reached over and squeezed Nat's hand. Gratefully, Nat squeezed back.

Nat muttered, "I am not having a good time."

"Gee, that's a bummer," Jenna replied, "because I was going to suggest we do this for the camp reunion this year."

They both snorted.

"I'll try the cell again," Clarissa announced.

Nat held her breath. It would be so cool if it worked.

"Darn," Clarissa said after a moment. "No go. Okay, let's call again for Chelsea. One, two, three..."

"Chelsea!" Nat and Jenna could barely make a sound, but Clarissa's voice was clear and strong.

No answer.

"Let's try Belle. One, two, three..."

"Belle!"

Nothing times two.

"The fog will lift," Clarissa said. "This way we can rest."

"Did I mention that Clarissa's a little too perky on occasion?" Jenna whispered to Nat. Nat chuckled ruefully.

About a minute passed. "Clarissa?" Jenna said. "I have to go to the bathroom. I'll be right back, okay?"

"Jenna, can't you wait?" Clarissa asked.

"No. I can't. I've already been waiting for ever. I won't go very far. Just...far enough."

Nat heard Jenna's movements as she left the log. She waved her hand through the fog, wishing she could clear it away so they could leave.

"Jenna?" Clarissa called.

"I'm fine," Jenna squawked back.

Nat and Clarissa sat in silence.

"It's going to be okay, Natalie," Clarissa promised.

Nat tried to respond. But her throat was closed up and her hands were trembling. Her cheeks tingled. She was really scared.

Jenna came back and sat beside her. It was freaky not to be able to see Jenna even though she was right beside her. She gave Nat's hand a squeeze and Nat squeezed back.

"I'm freaking out," Nat confessed.

Jenna squeezed her hand again.

"I mean, I am seriously about to lose it."

Again, Jenna squeezed her hand. Nat smiled weakly. She wished Jenna would say something – anything – to allay her fears.

Then suddenly, out of nowhere, a voice came out of the thick. "Guys?" It was Belle!

"Oh, thank goodness!" Nat cried happily. "Belle!" She squeezed Jenna's hand and jumped up, waving her hands even though it was pointless because of the thick fog. But she was just so incredibly relieved!

"Belle, here!" Nat and Clarissa shouted. Or Clarissa shouted and Nat squawked. "Here!"

"Belle!" Jenna croaked.

And Jenna sounded as if she were several metres away – too far away to have been holding hands with Natalie.

"Jenna?" Nat shrieked. "Where are you?"

"On my way, Goode," Jenna got out, still far away. "Belle! Belle!"

"Wait. If you're over there, then who was holding my hand?" Nat cried. She lurched through the fog and crashed her forehead into something hard.

Cropsy!

She realized a split second before she started screaming that it was a tree trunk.

"Ow!" she moaned. "Ow, ow, ow!"

"Natalie, are you all right?" Clarissa shouted.

"Natalie? Jenna?" Belle said. "Clarissa?"

"There's someone here!" Nat tried to warn them. "Someone who's not one of us! And it was holding my hand!"

Then she whacked her head on an overhanging branch.

And something came crashing through the forest.

CHAPTER ELEVEN

Alex's heart pounded. Her stomach literally turned over, and the blood raced through her body as she screamed bloody murder. She couldn't believe the horror of what was happening to her. The one-armed man in the hockey mask — Alex could now tell by his size that he was a man — dropped the chainsaw and ran towards her as she quickly staggered backwards, deeper into icy Shadow Lake.

"It's okay. I won't hurt you," he said as he reached up and wrapped his hand around the crosshatched mask. But before Alex could even see what the guy was doing with his hand, she let out another scream.

"It's okay," he repeated as he lifted the mask to reveal his face. Brown hair, hazel eyes, about eighteen years old...Alex recognized him immediately, but she couldn't quite place him. She did notice, thankfully, that he had *two* arms — the left one was cinched tightly

182

in a sling across his chest. He wasn't Cropsy, but who knew what other crazed maniac he might be?

"Hey, what the heck is going on?" she challenged him.

"Look, don't worry, I'll explain everything in a minute," he answered, but his eyes were focused far beyond Alex. He ran to the edge of the water and waved his arms back and forth.

"There's a hole in your boat!" he shouted, trying to get the attention of the girls in the boat.

"*What?*" Alex gasped, turning around. But the fog had swallowed up the boat, and she couldn't see it anywhere.

"You have a hole in your boat!" he boomed again across the water.

There was no answer.

"They can't hear you," Alex said. "They don't have any oars and they can't get back to shore!"

"I know. Come on." He grabbed her hand and pulled her back to land.

The eighteen-year-old guy let go of her once they were out of the lake and ran to the other boat. Alex hurried to keep pace. Her legs were numb and she felt a little dizzy, and by the time she reached him, he was pushing the boat through the sandy dirt and into the water.

"Come on, come on," he said. "We can row out and get them."

"Do you have oars?"

"Yes. Hurry!"

She splashed back into the water after him. Then he helped her climb in and sit on the wooden bench in the centre.

As the boat bobbed on the surface, he climbed in. It rocked from his weight, then smoothed out as he plopped down beside Alex.

"Here," the guy said. He reached under the seat and handed her a life jacket. "Put this on." It seemed to be the only one, but Alex took it.

While she put on the jacket, he hefted one of the oars from the floor and tried to slide it through the brass oarlock on the left. She stopped to help him, wrapping both her hands around the oar and guiding it through.

"Thanks," he gritted. "I broke my stupid arm in an accident."

Together they threaded the second oar into the right oarlock.

"Do you know how to row? I'm going to need some help."

"Sure," she said, taking up her oar.

"Let's sync up. One, two. One, two."

They moved the oars together, pushing them back, dipping them into the water. Pushing them back, dipping them into the water.

"That's good," he commented. "Let's keep that rhythm."

"Okay." She craned her neck over her shoulder. Her flashlight, still on, was nestled in her lap. She couldn't see the other boat. Couldn't hear it, either.

"I'm Jeremiah Wheatly," he said. "My family owns the ice-cream store in town." He paused. "Is Clarissa in that boat?"

"*Oh.*" She remembered now that they'd been teasing about him crushing on Clarissa at the cookout. Had that only been yesterday? Amazing.

"No," she said. She made a face at him. "You are so dead."

"We were coming to work on the boats and we heard you guys," he confessed. "We were going to scare you for fun."

"Fun?" she repeated, glaring at him.

"Yeah." He sighed. "I guess it wasn't all that fun."

"We?" she continued, ignoring his indirect apology.

"My friend Dan." He shook his head. "I'm really sorry. Can everybody swim?"

"Yes," she said. She took a deep breath. "Is that boat actually going to sink?"

"I don't know," he replied honestly. "With that much weight in it, it might."

"Guys! We're coming!" she shouted.

"Girls!" he yelled. "Camp Lakeview girls!"

There was no answer. She looked at Jeremiah. "Oh no, do you think they already sank?"

"I don't think it would happen that fast," he said. "But let's row faster, okay?"

She mirrored his movements as his muscles worked through his thin white T-shirt. The fog churned around the boat and they moved into it, then through it, and out into a thinner patch.

"Hello!" he yelled. "Can you hear me?"

Still nothing.

Jeremiah exhaled and glanced over his shoulder, lifting his oar out of the water. "Look around with your flashlight, okay?"

She did as he asked. Mostly the beam bounced off other patches of fog. She didn't see her friends anywhere.

"Girls!" Jeremiah cried. "Where are you?"

He sighed again, and glanced over his other shoulder. "The current is so fast."

"So? Is there something else?" Alex asked him suspiciously. "Something you're not telling me?"

He looked straight at her, and she felt a chill along her spine. "Yes," he admitted.

She licked her lips. What more could there be?

He took a moment. She waited.

"Our boat – and theirs – is headed towards Dead Man's Falls," he said.

Alex blinked at him. "Dead Man's *what*?"

"There are three main waterfalls on Shadow Lake. Ghost Falls, Skeleton Falls and Dead Man's Falls," he said. "Ghost Falls goes into a pool, and Skeleton Falls is further up the lake. But Dead Man's Falls..." His features hardened, and he sucked in his cheeks as if he really didn't want to go on. "Dead Man's Falls is on this side of the lake. And it's well named."

She waited a beat. When he said nothing more, she said, "Because...?"

"Because if you get swept down into the headwater, you can get dashed against the rocks if you don't know what you're doing. And if you make it through *that*, the height of the drop could easily kill you."

She gasped, then covered her mouth. "Why aren't there any signs? Any warnings?"

"There are," he said. "You guys must not have noticed them. There's no boating permitted on this lake and, well, locals like us bend the rules because we know where it's safe." He looked like he wanted to kick himself. If he didn't do it, Alex would be happy to do it for him.

"What are we going to do?"

"Hopefully, row to them in time to stop them from going over," he said. "And stop us, too."

"How?"

He gestured with his head towards the bottom of the boat. "There's some rope down there," he said. "We'll see what we can do with it once we find them."

He didn't have a full-blown plan. She didn't know why she expected him to, but she was angry with him for not having one. Mostly she was just scared.

Make that beyond scared. Make that on another planet past scared.

She looked back at the shoreline. "Did you see *anyone* else when you chased us down here? Where's the rest of my bunk?"

"I don't know," he confessed. "Dan's dog got loose a while back so he went off after him."

She tried to think of a Plan B. No cellphone, no one else around...

"So...it's up to us," Alex said.

"It's up to us," he agreed.

"Hold up — I totally recognize that guy. He's the dude from the ice-cream shop," said Brynn.

"No way!" Priya said.

"No way!" Candace repeated.

"It's so crazy. What's he doing here?" Brynn said.

"I don't know. This is all so weird and screwed up," said Priya.

In the fog, on Shadow Lake, all four bunkmates kneeled on the floor of the boat, leaning over the sides as they scooped their hands through the water. They were trying to turn the boat around and get back to Alex and the ice-cream guy. They could only hope he was trustworthy.

But as they tried to make headway, the fog had completely surrounded them. Brynn wasn't even sure they were still heading towards the other boat. She hoped so, because it felt as if the dinghy was travelling at a good speed.

Then she realized that her knees were wet. They hadn't been wet a couple of seconds ago.

"Hey, is someone splashing?" she asked cautiously.

"No," Priya said. "It would be hard to splash water into the boat. These sides are pretty high."

"Not me," Candace said. "No splashing here."

"Not me, either," Alyssa added.

"Well, we're getting wet," Brynn said.

"You're right." Priya stopped scooping water. "Was there water in the boat when we left?"

"I don't think so," Brynn said.

"I don't think there was," Candace added.

"We're taking on water," Alyssa concluded.

"Then…maybe there's a hole in the boat." Bending down, Brynn pressed her numb hands against the floor. There was more water than there had been even ten seconds ago. Her chest tightened and her heart went into overdrive. "Oh no, we're going to sink!"

"Do you feel the hole?" Alyssa said.

"No! No, I don't," Brynn wailed. "Oh, help…"

"Wait. Don't panic. Maybe we can find it and plug it up," Alyssa soothed her.

"With what?" Brynn asked. Frantic, she kept feeling for the hole. The water was so cold it felt like it was biting the backs of her hands.

"One of our shoes?" Candace ventured. "I'll donate one of mine."

Brynn heard shuffling; then something brushed against her elbow. Her hand wrapped around a wet sneaker.

"Thanks, Candace," Brynn replied.

Brynn was trying very hard not to panic, but they were out on the lake with no way to steer or move themselves, and their boat was taking on water. She wondered how deep the lake was. Some of the girls had gone in up to their necks that afternoon, and they had been very close to shore. She supposed it got deeper further out. But maybe she was wrong.

I really don't want to find out.

"Alyssa, call for Alex," she said. "Their boat's probably fine. Everybody, point your flashlights straight up. Maybe she'll be able to see them more easily."

"Alex!" Alyssa yelled. "Alex, Alex, Alex!"

They did as she asked, creating a beam that Brynn hoped would be visible through the fog. Maybe that guy with Alex had been able to call for help. Maybe he had extra life jackets, or some kind of plug, or something to bail with. Or an outboard motor, even.

Then her hand brushed a lumpy wet bundle covered with a light canvas material. Running her hands over it like a blind person, she found the Velcro straps across the front, the two armholes...

"Guys!" Brynn squeaked triumphantly. "I think I found a life jacket!" Eagerly, she felt around with her left hand. There was another life jacket there, too.

"I found another one. Check around for more."

"Okay, on it," Alyssa told her.

As Brynn listened to the sounds of the search, *more* water sloshed in the bottom of the boat.

I know how to swim, she reminded herself. *And so does everyone else. It's one of the things we learn at camp.*

"Nothing," Alyssa said. "No jacket."

"Same here," Priya said. "Nothing."

"I didn't find anything, either," Candace reported.

"Two life jackets are good," Brynn said, but she was disappointed.

Hey, we can swim.

In the fog.

In the dark.

In Shadow Lake.

CHAPTER TWELVE

Deep in the woods, smothered in fog, someone — or something — kept crashing through the forest. Jenna hugged herself, trying to make herself as small as possible, even though she kept walking into trees and rocks as she stumbled around. She didn't know which way to go.

"Belle?" she rasped. She could barely utter a syllable with her sore, hoarse throat.

"Girls, where are you?" Clarissa cried, sounding far away.

"I'm here!" Natalie yelled, her voice squeaking. "Is Chelsea with you?"

"No," Belle said. "Clarissa, where is everybody?"

"Listen to me, listen!" Natalie pleaded. "Someone else is here. Someone held my hand. I thought it was Jenna, but it wasn't!"

"Calm down, Natalie. It's just one of the other girls,

right, Clarissa?" Belle said. "Alex, or Alyssa—"

"No, Belle," Clarissa replied, her voice floating over the fog. "It's just Natalie, Jenna and me."

"*You left the others alone?*" Belle thundered.

Clarissa's answer was drowned out by the crashing as it grew louder.

Closer.

Jenna was totally freaking out. She stumbled against a tree and wrapped her arms around it to shield herself, but the noises seemed to be coming from everywhere at once. Her heart was pounding so hard it was about to shatter her ribcage, and she kept twisting around, staring into nothing but a thick cloud of white.

"It's Cropsy!" Natalie cried. "He's after us!"

"Are there bears?" Belle yelled.

"No! No bears," Clarissa replied. Then Jenna distinctly heard her mutter, "I hope."

What? Bears! Jenna blinked her eyes rapidly. Her breath was coming in short bursts. She felt dizzy, hot and cold. Her knees gave way and she fell to the ground, scrabbling to keep hold of her tree.

Through the blankets of white, something howled, high and crazy and angry. It wasn't human, and it wasn't a bear, and it was coming straight at Jenna.

She whimpered, eyes darting left, right, unable to see.

"Go away! I'm armed!" Belle yelled.

"Go! Shoo!" Clarissa joined in.

"Run! Everyone run!" Natalie croaked. "It's Cropsy!"

Jenna went cold all over. Her face was icy, her spine stiff and frozen. She was rooted to the spot, and she was trembling, as if someone had just thrown her into icy Shadow Lake. Dazed, she could hear the others yelling and shouting, trying to frighten their attacker away. Whatever it was, it wasn't the least bit afraid.

It was bounding closer, closer still...

Jenna gripped the tree trunk hard and thought of her brothers and her sister, and her mom and her dad. She started to cry.

I'm going to die, she thought. *It's going to kill me.*

Then something knocked Jenna down and drooled hot liquid on her face. Flailing her arms and kicking her legs, she remembered the part of the Cropsy story where he choked Randy into unconsciousness. Was that about to happen to her? Was that blood? Hot breath panted against her face as something held her down.

"Help!" she whispered. Then the thing backed off and started to...

...*bark?*

"Jenna!" Belle shouted.

"Monster!" a voice called. "Here, boy! It's okay. It's my dog."

A flashlight beam played in the fog, heading towards Jenna. Then the weight on top of Jenna lifted and crashed away.

Footfalls sounded from several directions, and Jenna slowly got to her feet. She lurched forwards, her heart pounding, watching more flashlight beams cast wide angles in the thick mist. She flailed through the fog like the mummy in the old monster movies.

"Belle! I'm over here!" she pleaded. "Clarissa! Nat!"

"I can't see you," Belle said.

"Follow my voice," said the intruder. "The fog's thinner up here. You'll be able to see."

I'm not moving, Jenna thought. Her legs were shaking. She took a step forward and collapsed.

Then leaves shuffled directly behind her. A twig snapped.

She whirled around.

"Jenna?" It was Natalie.

"Nat!" Jenna threw open her arms and they hugged each other tightly. "Who is that guy? What's going on?"

"Come on up here," said the voice.

"Hold on." That was Belle. "Who are you? And what were you doing just now to my campers?"

"My name is Dan Magnusen, and I – *ouch!*"

"I've got him, girls," Belle said. "He's telling the truth as far as the fog goes. Follow my voice and you'll get out of that really thick stuff."

"Jenna, I don't want to move. I don't think I *can*," Natalie said.

"Me neither," Jenna confessed. "I thought...I thought he was Cropsy."

"I did, too."

"Girls?" Belle called.

"We're here," Natalie squeaked.

Footfalls sounded through the undergrowth. Natalie and Jenna squeezed each other fearfully. It was very, very hard for Jenna not to bolt and run away.

"It's me," Clarissa said.

Jenna let go of Natalie with one hand and flailed in the fog. "Here, we're here!" she breathed.

A hand wrapped around hers. "Got you," Clarissa said. "Got you too, Natalie. Come on."

"Clarissa?" Natalie said. "It's really you, right?"

"It's really me. Belle? I've got them."

"Follow the sound of my voice," Belle said.

The three moved carefully. Jenna trembled with each step. She moved jerkily, like a string puppet, as if she had forgotten how to walk. Natalie was shaking like a leaf. She was holding onto Jenna's hand so tightly that Jenna was beginning to lose feeling in her fingers.

But as they climbed their way up the slope, sure enough, the fog began to thin. She could make out vague shapes – trees, and someone or something standing off in the distance.

As they trudged higher, she could see much better. Belle was behind a guy – Dan – who looked about high-school-senior age, with blond hair and a little goatee. And he only had one arm!

Then she saw that Belle had actually yanked Dan's other arm around his body and was holding onto it like a kung fu fighter.

"Are you two okay?" she asked Jenna and Natalie.

"Yes," they said at the same time.

Then a waist-high, golden-haired dog bounded from among the trees and galloped up to Dan, chuffing and sniffing at him. It sat back on its haunches and cocked its head at Belle. It growled softly.

"It's okay, Monster," Dan said. His voice was a little familiar. "I'm from town. You've probably seen me, if you've been to Camp Lakeview before. I work at Wheatly's Waffle Cones."

"How do you know we're from Camp Lakeview?" Belle asked him, still locking his arm behind his body. Before he could answer, she said, "Did that dog hurt either of you? Bite you?"

"No." But now she knew what the hot liquid was. *Yuck.* Jenna lifted up her T-shirt and tried to wipe the dog slobber off her face without showing her bra.

Dan shifted uncomfortably in Belle's grip, but the counsellor didn't ease up on him. There sure was more to Belle than met the eye. She had to be some kind of martial arts expert. And she was pretty fearless. Jenna wondered if she was carrying a gun. She'd said she was armed.

She was very, very glad that Belle was her counsellor.

"Answer my question," Belle said, jerking Dan's arm. "How do you know we're from Camp Lakeview? Have you done something to my other campers?"

"*Ow.*" He rose up on his tiptoes. "We listened in on your campfire."

Belle's voice was even sharper. "*We?*"

"Jeremiah and me. We heard you guys talking about Cropsy and we decided to try to scare you." He looked like he wanted the ground to open up and swallow him.

Jenna wished she could make that happen.

"A joke," Belle echoed disdainfully. "All this for a joke. You are in so much trouble." She looked left, right. "Tell this Jeremiah to show himself. Joke's over."

Dan bit his lower lip between his teeth. "Well, ah, he's with the others."

"What others? How many of you *are* there?" Clarissa asked, sounding uneasy.

"Oh, there's just two of us," Dan said. "I mean, the others...of *you.*"

"He's at the campsite?" Belle asked him. "*Our* campsite?"

"Scaring our campers?" Clarissa said.

"I'm sorry," Dan said. "I was going to go with him, but Monster got loose. We had him in the truck, but he got out."

"How were you going to scare them?" Even though she released him, Belle looked like she was about to punch him in the face.

"With a chainsaw and a hockey mask. But that's all," Dan assured her, and he sounded embarrassed and frightened himself as he rubbed his arm and flexed his hand. "I'm sorry. Really."

"Not as sorry as you're going to be." Belle ran her hands through her black hair. "Clarissa, you never should have left the girls alone."

"I know." She hung her head. "I'm really sorry, Belle. We were worried about you and Chelsea. We were just going to look for a few minutes and we got lost."

"Did *you* find her?" Jenna asked hopefully.

"No." Belle exhaled. She looked at Dan. "How about you, scary guy? Did you see a girl with blonde hair leave our campsite? Did you see where she went?"

He shook his head. "I'm sorry, no. We must have left before then."

Belle whipped her cellphone out of her shorts and punched in numbers. "I'm calling the police. They're State Troopers here, right?" She glared at Dan.

"Right," he said.

Maybe because of the distress in his master's voice, Monster chuffed and trotted over to Dan. Dan absently rubbed Monster's head between his ears.

"Okay, wait a minute," Natalie said to him. "You *were* down by the waterfall, right? Holding my hand?"

"What?" Dan asked. "No. I've been up here the whole time."

"What's the matter?" Belle asked, sliding a glance towards Natalie as she pressed her phone against her ear.

"I *told* you," Natalie wailed. Her eyes welled. "Someone was holding my hand. I thought it was Jenna, but then she was too far away. So then I was hoping... Jenna, was it you after all?" Natalie pleaded. "After you went to the bathroom...please, if you pranked me somehow..."

"Nat, I wish I could tell you it was me," Jenna said. "But it wasn't."

Jenna, Clarissa and Natalie traded anxious looks. Belle was scowling at Dan, absolutely livid.

"Maybe Mister Dan's still trying to playing a funny little joke," she said harshly. "Call your friend out. *Now*."

"He's not here," Dan insisted. Belle waited, glaring at him, her phone against her ear. "Okay. I'll try. Jer! Jeremiah!" he bellowed. Monster began to bark.

They all waited.

"Jeremiah!" he yelled again.

Monster howled and danced.

"Hush," Dan said to the dog. "See?" he said to Belle. "He's not in this part of the woods."

She said in a booming voice, "Jeremiah, if you are out here with us and you don't show yourself immediately, I will have you arrested."

There was silence.

She gestured for everyone to start moving. "My phone isn't working," Belle told Dan. "Give me yours. You must have one?"

"Yeah." As they walked, he fished in his pocket and handed it to Belle. "But it never works up here."

Belle punched the buttons and listened. She made a face and shook her head.

"No signal," she reported. She gave Dan a look. "I'll just keep this for now."

202

She looked over her shoulder at Natalie, Jenna and Clarissa. "Hurry. Stick together. We're hustling back to the campsite, *now*."

"What about Chelsea?" Jenna asked her, working to keep up with Belle.

"After I know everyone else is safe, I'll look for her some more," Belle said, shining her flashlight over every centimetre of forest ahead and to the sides of them.

Jenna was more afraid than she had ever been in her life. If Natalie was right, there was someone in the woods besides them, Jeremiah and Dan. Someone who was not one of them.

Please, please let it be his stupid friend Jeremiah, Jenna prayed.

"I have a truck," Dan told Belle. "There's a market a few kilometres down the road. They have a pay phone."

Belle dipped her head. "Thank goodness," she murmured.

Without warning, a jag of lightning stabbed the darkness. Thunder rumbled in response. The skies broke open, and it began to rain. Hard. And cold.

"Keep going!" Belle shouted. "Don't stop!"

* * *

The rain splattered on the tree trunks and the boulders, creating slippery gullies in the soft earth. Jenna slipped and nearly lost her balance several times. Each time, she managed to grab onto a branch or steady herself against a rock. Once, Clarissa grabbed her hand just before she went down. And another time, Natalie helped her. But she was definitely feeling shaky.

"We're almost there," Dan shouted over his shoulder as he walked at the head of the line.

Then Monster whined. He snorted and looked at Jenna, sidling up to her so that his soaking wet fur brushed against her leg.

"Oh no," Natalie whispered. She grabbed Jenna's hand. "It's Cropsy."

The dog whined again and began to whimper; he danced sideways, stopped, and backed up, running into Jenna.

"Hey!" Jenna yelled. "Dan! Something's wrong with Monster."

"Monster, come!" Dan summoned him.

The dog's hackles rose. Instead of bounding over to Dan, he stood deathly still and began to growl into the shuttered darkness of the woods.

*   *   *

Something dripped onto the back of Chelsea's head. Something cold and wet.

Her eyes flickered open. She was lying face down on something soft, lumpy and terribly dusty. The dust was fast becoming mud. Was it a mattress? Was she in her bunk at Camp Lakeview? Had she been having a dream?

That can't be right, she thought. *We have nice clean mattresses, and it doesn't rain indoors.*

Confused and half-awake, she tried to raise her head, but she was too woozy. She closed her eyes again and took a deep breath of moist, muddy air. She coughed.

Her ankle was throbbing. The drips came hard and fast.

It's raining, she realized.

She shifted her weight, rocking back and forth, and managed to roll over onto her back. As she slowly raised her hand over her face, the rain cascaded onto her cheeks and forehead. The cloud-choked moon glistened through a jagged hole about five metres above her, and she remembered that the ground had given way beneath her feet.

I fell...onto a mattress?

Her blood ran cold.

Whose mattress?

She turned her head.

205

Noooooo!

Chelsea screamed – or she would have, if she hadn't been so hoarse.

Moonlight and raindrops streamed down onto the bandaged profile of a human body swathed in a sheet. It was a man, lying limp on a large wooden table. Thick wires were attached to his head and his arms. He wasn't moving. The sheet was wet, outlining his body – chest, sunken stomach and legs.

She stuffed her hands in her mouth to keep herself from screaming. What had happened to him? Was he dead? A thousand questions shot through her mind. It took a few seconds to realize that she was panting and crawling backwards, putting as much distance between herself and the man as possible. She couldn't feel the pain in her ankle. She couldn't feel anything. She was shaking violently. Her stomach contracted and her mouth filled with acid. She clenched her lips and she started crying and shaking her head from side to side. But she couldn't stop staring at him.

What's wrong with him? Is he...is he...

"Hey," she whispered. "Mister, are you hurt?"

As she crawled backwards, her foot smacked up against something hard. She jerked around on her hands and knees.

She let out a hoarse cry.

It was another man, this one strapped into a wooden chair. It was one of the thick chair legs that she'd hit. His eyes were closed, his head lolling to one side. There was a metal saucer that might have once been clamped over his head, but it had come unfastened and hung a few centimetres above him. His face was half gone, rotted away, revealing white bone beneath. His mouth hung open. She could see only blackness inside, no teeth.

Leather straps bound his wrists and ankles and crossed his chest. He was wearing a light-coloured shirt and what looked to be jeans, tattered and dusty.

Chelsea's mouth worked, but no more sound would come out. Then she heard a noise from behind her and whirled around again.

A beady-eyed rat was perched on the shrouded man's soaked chest. Its red eyes gleamed in the moonlight, and when it saw Chelsea, it rose up on its hind legs and squeaked as the rain fell down on it. Then it skittered onto the man's face.

The man still didn't move.

"Shoo! Shoo!" Chelsea hissed at it, scrambling towards it and waving her right arm. "Get off him!"

The rat squeaked again. Then it dropped off the man and onto the ground, which was covered with old newspapers, dusty fast-food cartons and animal droppings. A soda can rolled when the rat knocked it.

The creature stopped, sat up again, and stared right at her. It squeaked.

It scurried straight for her.

Whimpering, Chelsea crawled backwards again. She ran into the man strapped into the chair, only this time she connected with his leg. It gave way.

With a strangled cry, she grabbed a wad of dripping newspaper and threw it at the rat.

It squeaked, turned tail, and darted into the shadows.

Then a horrible electrical buzzing shattered the air. The wires attached to the man on the table began to jerk and dance.

The man in the chair jerked too, his arms and legs vibrating wildly as the noise grew louder. It was horrible, like power lines snapping, zinging and crackling. He vibrated harder. The noise got louder still, piercing Chelsea's eardrums.

A flash of lightning shot across the hole in the ceiling.

The eyes of the man in the chair burst open.

And the figure on the table sat up.

CHAPTER THIRTEEN

"No!" Valerie croaked as she, Tori and Gaby ran into another dead end.

They had no idea where they were. When the rain had started coming down, they'd turned right around, thinking they were headed back to the campsite. But somewhere along the line they'd made a huge mistake, and now they kept running into little inlets surfaced with rock. It was like being in a funhouse, without the fun.

"Belle! Chelsea!" Gaby yelled. She stomped her foot, sending mud flying upwards onto her shins. She didn't care. Getting muddy was the least of their problems.

"One, two, three," Tori said.

"Belle! Chelsea!" they squealed. "Clarissa!"

"We're too hoarse," Gaby said. "The rain's too loud."

"What are we going to do?" Valerie asked. Her teeth were chattering. "I'm freezing."

"We all are." Tori pushed her locks of hair out of her face. "Let's keep going."

"Going? Where? Where is it that we're going?" Gaby demanded. "We're just getting more and more lost!"

"What do you suggest?" Valerie asked, getting in Gaby's face. "That we stand here all night until we catch pneumonia?"

"Yes! No!" Gaby fought back tears. "I don't know. I don't know what to do!"

"I say we keep going," Valerie insisted. "Maybe we'll find a cave or something."

"I can't believe this." Tori shined her flashlight into the raindrops. "I hate this."

"You're not alone." Valerie gave Tori a quick hug. Then she hesitated, and gave Gaby one, too.

"Oh, look," Gaby muttered. "We're *bonding*."

But the truth was, she really needed that hug. So after she held herself stiffly for a moment, she hugged Valerie back. Then Tori.

"Wow, we *are* bonding," Valerie said.

The three smiled weakly.

"Let's keep going," Gaby said. She aimed her flashlight into the blackness. A flash of lightning revealed a space between two thick pines.

"In there," she suggested. "Maybe the trees can keep the rain off."

"Maybe," Tori said, showing them her crossed fingers.

They headed for the trees.

"Bail faster!" Brynn whispered through the stinging rain, lightning and thunder, as Candace, Priya and Alyssa made cups out of their hands and tried to get rid of the water that was filling up the boat. A hole in the bottom, rainwater on the top, plus the combined weight of the four of them...it was just too much for the boat to handle.

Plus, they were freezing. Seriously.

They kept yelling for Alex, but the rain made a terrible racket against the surface of the lake. As patches of fog wafted past them, Brynn squinted through the white billows, searching with her flashlight for Alex, or even better, for land. Clouds covered the moon, and she didn't see any lights anywhere. Maybe no one lived around here. What about other campers? Were they truly up here all alone, except for the ice-cream guy?

Despite being seated so deep in the icy water, their boat rushed along – or so it felt – like the inner tubes at WetWorld, where they had gone on a camp-sponsored field trip two summers before. That had been their first experience with Gaby, who had intimidated Grace into cutting in line and disobeying their chaperones. No one had liked her. Now Brynn found herself hoping that Gaby was all right – safe, warm and out of this rain. She hoped that for everyone, including Chelsea.

"Why are we moving so fast?" Candace asked. "We don't have lakes like this back home."

"Maybe we're going towards some kind of run-off place," Alyssa said.

"Oh. Freaky," Candace replied.

They grew silent. Kneeling, Brynn was up to her thighs in water.

"Guys, listen," Brynn said. "The boat is overloaded. It's in danger of sinking. We have to lighten the load."

"But there's nothing in the boat we can get rid of," Priya said. "I mean, we could probably pull the little bench seat off and toss it, but it doesn't weigh much."

"Right," Brynn said. She was quiet for a few beats.

"*Oh*," Candace said.

Brynn waited a couple more seconds to see if the other two would figure out what she was trying to say. But no one said anything. She was going to have to.

"We have two life vests," she began. "We should pick our two strongest swimmers and they can hold onto the boat while the other two try to keep it bailed out."

"Hold onto...you mean, get out of the boat and *swim*?" Alyssa asked.

"You can't be serious," Priya insisted, her voice shaky and uncertain. "Alex!" she started yelling, straining her voice. "We need you *now*! Show us where you are!"

"Show us where *we* are!" Alyssa cried.

"I am serious," Brynn said as the others sighed and slumped dejectedly back into the boat. "I wish I had a better idea, but if you do, please tell us what it is. So far, this makes the most sense. Whoever swims can hold onto the side of the boat. Someone in the boat could hold onto her wrists to make sure she doesn't lose her grip."

"But it's so cold in the lake. And what if one of the swimmers *does* let go of the boat? Or the person in the boat lets go?" Priya asked. "If we drift into another thick patch of fog, we might not be able to find her and rescue her."

"And she might go down and drown in Shadow Lake," Candace murmured.

"Not with a life vest on," Alyssa said. "They'll keep the swimmers afloat."

"Oh no," Candace whispered.

"I'm sorry," Brynn said earnestly. "I can't think of anything else to do. If no one wants to volunteer, we can do something like pick numbers, or do rock, paper, scissors..."

"I'll go," Alyssa volunteered. "I'm a very good swimmer."

"Me too," Candace said.

Dear, sweet Candace. Brynn actually smiled.

"No offence," Brynn said to Candace, "I *would* call you a very good swimmer." She licked her lips and raised her chin. "But I'm a *better* swimmer."

"I..." Candace hugged herself. "You're an excellent swimmer, Brynn. But I'm scared. I don't want to do this, and I don't want *you* to do this."

"I don't like this, either," Priya said. "I'm a good swimmer too. But this is dangerous."

"Well, I'm not concerned about that right now. Candace, please, give me your life jacket," Brynn insisted.

Brynn heard the *rrrip* of Velcro as Candace took off her life jacket. Alyssa was already wearing the other one.

As Brynn slid on the jacket and began to buckle it across her chest, her heart hammered and her hands shook. She tried hard not to think about the ghost story Tori had told them. What kind of things bobbed beneath the surface of the vast, dark lake?

She hadn't shared the story Sarah had told her about the school bus. The story said that one winter, a school bus filled with children had veered off the highway and plummeted into the waters of Lake Michigan. It plunged to the icy bottom of the lake, where it was so cold that the bodies froze...and to that day, the bus sat on the bottom...except for when the lake waters churned...and then it bobbed to the surface, where waterskiers and boaters saw the terrified, blue faces before the bus sank again.

"We should sit on the sides and fall backwards at the same time," Alyssa said.

"No way," Brynn argued. "I want someone holding onto us at all times."

"Brynn," Alyssa began, "there's no other way to get out quickly. And if we *don't* get out quickly, we could sink the boat. We're both good swimmers. We can do this."

"No, wait," Candace said. She took a breath and wrapped her hand around Brynn's fingers. "Please, don't do it. I'm so scared."

"It'll be okay," Brynn said, giving her a squeeze, but she felt like a total liar. She had no idea if it would be okay. For all she knew, either she or Alyssa could hit their heads on a rock or something floating by, get knocked out, and drown.

It happens. People die, she thought. *Then other people make up ghost stories about them.*

She let go of Candace's hand.

"Okay, Alyssa, let's do it."

They sat on opposite sides of the boat, facing each other. Brynn was grateful for the break in the fog. She wasn't sure she would have the nerve to do this if she couldn't see anything.

"Okay, on my count," Alyssa said. "One, two, *three!*"

Brynn fell backwards into the water.

It was so cold it took her breath away. For one panicky moment she thought she was going to shoot straight to the bottom, but the buoyant life jacket did its job. She bobbed upright and shot both her hands towards Candace, who grabbed them and wrapped them around the side of the boat.

"Alyssa, are you okay?" Brynn shouted.

"I'm good," Alyssa said on the other side of the boat.

"I've got her," Priya announced.

"It's actually kind of refreshing," Alyssa added, her teeth chattering crazily. "It's so darn hot tonight."

Brynn smiled with semi-numb lips. "You know, you're right."

She pulled herself up to peer into the boat. She couldn't see the water level, but she knew it was still too high.

"Okay, guys, keep bailing," she said. As her legs dangled in the water, she formulated a quick plan in the event that the boat filled up with too much water to stay afloat – she would give Candace back the life jacket, and Candace and Priya would also get out. Then the four of them would flip the boat over. The hull would float, and all four of them could hang onto it.

"Wow, I can really feel the boat moving," Alyssa said. "We're definitely going somewhere."

Alyssa was right. That gave Brynn pause. She wasn't much of a nature person, but she figured that if the lake waters were flowing towards a point...

It could be a point like a waterfall. Her stomach did a flip.

Or it could be some kind of run-off drain, she thought, *with a big grate that will hold us back.* That would be a good thing.

Oh, please, please, let it be a grate.

Then something bumped against her ankle. She cried out and kicked her legs.

"What's wrong?" Candace cried, holding onto her hands more tightly.

It bumped against her again. "Something's touching me!" she shouted.

"Oh, Brynn," Candace moaned. "Get back in the boat!"

"It could be a fish," Alyssa said. "There're fish in lakes."

"Right," Brynn said. But her eyes were welling with

tears because she was so frightened. She wondered if there were eels in lakes, too. She thought about the Lake Michigan school bus and imagined one of the passengers reaching a cold hand through an open window, trying to get out of the bus...or pull her into it.

Stop it, she admonished herself. *Pull yourself together. This is just a lake.*

Something nudged her other ankle.

She screamed.

Alex was feeling more light-headed and disoriented as she and Jeremiah rowed through the storm. The boat bounced on choppy waves, adding to her nausea.

I need some sugar, she thought.

"You're slowing down," Jeremiah said.

"Do you have anything to eat?" she asked him. "Something sweet?"

"Man, I wish," he said. "I'm hungry. We have some sandwiches in the truck."

She closed her eyes and thought about the insulin kit back in her tent. She wished she had thought to grab it. She wished she'd given herself an injection earlier in the evening, when Chelsea thought she had.

As a bolt of lightning jagged overhead, he turned his head and looked hard at her. "Are you okay?"

She began to nod, and then she shook her head. "I'm a diabetic," she said. "If something...happens..." She swallowed. She had to be clear with him. "If I happen to faint—"

"Oh, man," he said, sounding frightened.

"Listen to me," she said.

They both stopped rowing and he hung over his oar, giving her his full attention.

"If I faint, get me something sweet as soon as possible. A candy bar, a soda, anything. Okay? After we...don't go over the waterfall?"

"Oh, man," he whispered, this time to himself.

She looked at him hard. "You have to promise, Jeremiah. Will you try your best?"

Her look must have steadied him. He took a deep breath.

"Okay. I will. If you faint." He frowned. "You're not saying this to get back at me, are you? For scaring you guys?"

"I would never joke about something like diabetes," she said. *But some people would.* She thought of Chelsea.

I wonder where she went. I wonder what she's doing right now.

Despite her hurt feelings, Alex really did care.

"All this happened because of Chelsea. She's that girl who left first. People started leaving to go find her. Did you guys see her?"

"No," he said. "We were already gone. To get the... chainsaw." He exhaled. "We're stupid," he said. "Stupid, stupid, stupid."

"No argument here."

They rowed for a bit, and then he let his oar trail in the water. "Hey, shine your flashlight to the right."

She had the flashlight in her lap. She did as he asked, looking where he was looking, but seeing nothing.

"Do it again."

She did, squinting into the rain. If they'd been in a car, she would have told him to pull over until the rain stopped. Then it occurred to her that they might ram the other boat without realizing it.

Great. Something else to worry about.

Just then, she saw a faint yellow beam through the rain!

"You guys!" she cried. Waving her left arm, she steadied herself and half-rose.

"Stay down!" Jeremiah shouted.

So she sat down again and waved both hands. "Priya! Lyss! Candace! Brynn!" she yelled.

She heard them yelling and cheering. She waved her flashlight back and forth, back and forth, screaming as loudly as she could.

In the foggy darkness, they did the same.

"Yes!" she shrieked. "We're coming!"

"Keep the flashlight steady," he urged her. "We don't want to lose them in the water."

Another zigzag of lightning lit up the sky like fireworks, and she saw his huge grin.

But a wave of dizziness hit her hard, and her fingers loosened from around the black cylinder.

And with a plop, the flashlight fell into the lake.

Gaby ducked beneath a tree limb cracked lengthwise, which was spouting water like a rain gutter. She grabbed Valerie's arm. "Look," she said, pointing dead ahead.

Valerie stumbled beside her. Tori pulled up short.

All three of them stood frozen in the downpour. Then they backtracked into the bushes, peering around the branches at the black wide-body truck that sat silent and unmoving in the rain. It was facing away from the three girls.

"It's got to belong to whoever was chasing us in the woods," Tori said into Valerie's ear. In turn, Valerie repeated what Tori had said to Gaby, as if they were playing "Operator".

Gaby nodded. Valerie put her arms around herself, shivering, wondering what they should do. The truck lights were out. The doors were shut. Maybe the bad guy was in there, watching them in his rear-view mirror.

Maybe he was going to jump out at any second and chase them some more.

"Well, the good news is, I don't think Cropsy had a truck," Valerie said, trying to make a joke.

Gaby grunted. "That's not funny."

They watched for another minute or two. It seemed like for ever to Valerie as they huddled together in the rain. It was hard to believe that only this afternoon she had been too hot, and her biggest problem was that she'd been worried she'd have to sleep with Chelsea or Gaby when they drew lots for tents.

Between rolls of thunder, something crashed in the woods behind them. Valerie stiffened. The other girls heard it too. Gaby jerked and Valerie caught her breath.

"We should stay out of sight until we know what that is," Valerie said.

"Maybe it's us. Belle. 5A." Tori clasped her hands together and tilted her head back in the rain. "Oh please, oh please, oh please."

"Maybe it's not," Gaby said.

Tori unclasped her hands.

They crept quietly back the way they had come, then pushed away pine branches and took a few steps backwards, concealing themselves. By silent agreement, they turned off their flashlights.

Valerie hunkered down between Gaby and Tori, her view partially obscured by a thick tree trunk. Her heartbeat pounded in her forehead and neck. Her chest tightened; she was holding her breath and she couldn't make herself exhale.

They waited shoulder to shoulder. With her free hand, Gaby took Valerie's hand. Valerie had her flashlight in the other hand, or she would have passed the squeeze on to Tori, the way they were taught to do last year.

All three girls stood like statues. Valerie still couldn't breathe. She was beginning to get dizzy. As the rain pelted her eyelids, she forced herself to stare into the darkness, alert, engaging all her senses in case she had to protect herself.

Lightning crackled overhead, and she jumped. Gaby gave her hand a tight squeeze. Thunder roared like a lion. But then, seemingly out of nowhere, the fog lifted.

"Oh," Tori whispered.

It was a trio of deer. Beautiful and sleek, two does and a little fawn sauntered past, seemingly unaware of the girls. The three exhaled, Valerie hanging onto the trunk as she regained her composure.

"I don't think those deer would be so calm if there were humans coming right behind them," Valerie said after they had disappeared.

"They were calm around us, and we're humans," Gaby said.

"They didn't know we were here," Valerie shot back. "We weren't moving around. Do you hear anything now? No one is crashing through the forest."

"So you think it was the deer making all the noise?" Tori asked.

"I don't *hear* anything, but I *see* a truck," Gaby said.

"Maybe there're two teenagers inside, making out or something," Tori ventured.

"In a storm?" Valerie countered. "I can see it now. The two teens run out of gas. They're kissing, not realizing that Cropsy is about to yank open the truck door and murder them both..."

"Don't, okay?" Tori said. "I'm scared enough."

Valerie was about to apologize when lightning flashed and the side mirror glinted. She took a step forward.

Tori said, "What are you doing?"

"The rain will hide us," Valerie said. "If we sneak up on the truck now, at least we'll be able to see if there's anyone inside when the lightning flashes again. But if it stops raining..."

"Oh, no," Tori moaned. "Let's stay away from it."

"Tori, we're lost," Valerie said. "Maybe it's the truck of that guy who was chasing us. Maybe he's waiting out the storm to scare us some more. Or maybe it is teenagers kissing. But what if it's deserted, and someone left their keys in the ignition? If they left the keys, we can get out of here and go for help."

"I don't know how to drive," Gaby said. She looked at Valerie. "Do you?"

"Sort of," Valerie said. "I could fake it."

"I totally do," Tori announced. They looked at her. "Hey, LA girl here. A stunt guy taught me during a lull in Michael's dad's shoot."

"Hollywood, I love you," Gaby said.

"But there's a problem, chicks," Tori continued. "People don't leave their keys in their cars. That's just a movie thing."

"Some people do, too, out here in the country," Valerie insisted.

"She's right," Gaby said. "They do."

"That's incredible," Tori said. "That would *never* happen in LA. Okay, let's watch it for a little longer and see if anyone gets out."

"Why would they get out in the middle of a storm?" Gaby argued.

"Well, if there *are* bad guys in there, we can whap them over the head with our flashlights." Valerie looked at the other two. "There are three of us, and we're strong."

"You've got *that* right," Gaby said.

"I take Pilates," Tori announced. She flexed her bicep. "Check it out."

"We should keep our flashlights turned off," Valerie reminded them. "We'll have to move with the flashes of lightning and the moonlight."

"Oh, I can't believe this is happening," Tori moaned.

"Well, it is," Valerie said. "We'll take over the truck and drive to safety and report what's going on to the State Troopers."

"The police?" Tori said faintly.

"Yes, the police," Gaby said firmly. "People are missing, and someone was chasing us. This is *serious*."

There was a beat, as if Valerie was giving each girl time to change her mind. Then there was another flash of lightning, and Valerie shifted her weight. She didn't want to do it alone, but she was beginning to think she might have to.

"Oh, I don't know," Tori said.

"Tori, listen, we should stick together," Gaby said. "That's how we got messed up in the first place, by everybody going off in different directions. You're the one who knows how to drive. We need you."

"We'll put you in the middle for protection, and then we'll just sneak right up there," Valerie said.

"I'm never going camping again," Tori muttered. "From now on, it's hotels."

"So you'll do it," Valerie said.

"I'll do it," Tori agreed.

"Group hug," Gaby insisted.

"Gotta love the bonding," Valerie quipped, and they all laughed.

Bending down, they moved as stealthily and silently as they could, even though the rain was falling noisily and the rolls of thunder were deafening. Valerie listened hard for voices, music from a radio – anything to warn them that the truck was occupied. But she could hear nothing.

Then, just as abruptly as it had started, it stopped raining. There was one more rumble of thunder, and the storm was over.

Yikes, bad timing, Valerie thought, wincing as her shoes crunched on gravel. Beside her, Gaby put her finger to her lips. She pointed to her own feet, and Valerie saw that she was tiptoeing. Valerie did the same.

They reached the back of the truck, squatting so they couldn't be detected in the mirrors, and paused. Valerie couldn't imagine actually hitting anyone with a flashlight, but she carried it in her right hand, preparing herself just in case.

Tori, on the left, gestured that she would go along

the truck towards the driver's side. Valerie nodded, and indicated that Gaby should sneak over to the passenger's door on the right. She decided that she should go with Tori, because it was more likely that there was a driver than just a passenger inside.

Two flashlights over the head are better than one, she thought grimly.

She mouthed a count, and on three the girls bent way over and scooted from the back of the truck to the doors.

What if they're locked and someone is inside? Valerie wondered, but it was too late to do anything about that now.

Tori depressed the opening mechanism on her door handle. It clicked.

She blinked at Valerie. Then she yanked it and pulled it open and the two looked in, flashlights raised over their heads.

Deserted!

Gaby's door opened, too, and she climbed in and drew the door shut very quietly. Then she locked it.

"Look, there's no key," she said, leaning across the seat to touch the ignition.

"Oh, no," Tori murmured.

"Move, please," Valerie told Tori. She dropped to her knees – the gravel stung – and felt underneath the

228

side for one of those magnetic key holders, like her father had put on his Camry just in case.

Her hands brushed a plastic rectangle. Applying a little bit of effort, she pulled it off and slid back the lid. Sure enough, there was a key inside.

She held it up. "Ta-da!"

"You're the best!" Tori whispered, throwing her arms around Valerie.

Valerie climbed into the cab and scooted into the middle. Tori got in next and shut and locked the door, all in one terrified motion. Then she jammed the key into the ignition, pressed her foot on the gas, and turned it on. It roared to life.

"Here we go," she whispered. She put it in gear. The truck began to roll.

"Yesss," Gaby whispered.

Tori didn't turn on the headlights. *Smart move*, Valerie thought as she kept watch in the rear-view mirror for someone to tear out of the woods and race after them.

After they had driven in the dark for about three minutes, Valerie let out a strangled, hoarse whoop. Tori and Gaby did too.

"We did it! We rock!" Gaby rasped.

"We are so amazing!" Tori agreed.

They high-fived one another, laughing and squeaking.

"Should I turn on the lights now?" Tori asked them.

"Yes," Valerie said. "Unless they can run really fast, they won't be able to stop us from leaving. Now, let's go get some help for Bunk 5A!"

They laughed and cheered some more.

CHAPTER FOURTEEN

As the rain stopped, Monster the dog kept whining and growling at shadows.

"Easy, Monster. Down, boy," Dan urged him.

But the hair along Monster's back rose, his body tensing as he stared at something Nat couldn't see. The noises he made sounded very threatening.

"I don't like this. What's he growling at?" Belle asked Dan. She was walking beside him. Nat and Jenna were behind them, followed by Clarissa.

"He's a hunting dog. He probably hears some birds," Dan said. "Monster, here."

"Is it possible he's sensing Chelsea or some of the other girls?" Belle asked. She cupped her mouth with her hands. "Chelsea! Camp Lakeview! Can you hear me?"

There was no answer.

"I think we're almost back to the campsite," Clarissa

told Nat and Jenna with a hopeful smile. "We'll gather everybody and get to that market for some hot chocolate and something to eat."

"Okay," Nat said gratefully. She could hardly wait.

"What about our stuff?" Jenna asked.

"I don't care about our stuff. I'll buy you new stuff," Nat told her. "I just want to get out of here and I *never* want to go camping again!"

"I'm really sorry," Dan muttered. "Things just totally got out of hand."

"You've got that right," Belle snapped. "Chelsea!" she shouted. "5A!"

"I hope everybody else is still at the campsite," Jenna told Nat. "Chelsea, too. Once we find her, I'm going to give her all my candy *and* my cupcakes."

"I won't lose my temper around her ever again. And Gaby, too. I'll make sure this is the best summer they ever had."

"I'm so happy to hear that, girls," Clarissa said. "I'm sure Chelsea and Gaby will be too."

Nat blushed. She didn't mean for Clarissa to overhear them. But as she thought about it, she decided she was glad that she had. It would help Nat to remember her resolution.

"Thanks," Jenna said. She nodded and held up her right hand. "New leaf. That's a promise."

*   *   *

They kept slogging through the mud until, at last, Nat recognized their surroundings – the big bush and the granite boulder.

"We're back!" she cried. She and Jenna hugged and did a little dance as the group hustled to the campsite.

But there were no campers. Not one. There was no one in the tents.

"Oh, no," Belle moaned. She ran her hands through her hair as she climbed on the edge of the fire ring and cupped her hands around her mouth. "Camp Lakeview!" she bellowed, turning right, left, straight ahead. "Camp Lakeview!"

"Now what?" Clarissa said, as she picked up a flashlight that someone had dropped. "Where could they be?"

"Tell me again what you two were planning," Belle ordered Dan. "Walk me through the whole thing."

"Okay. We listened to you from up there." He shone his flashlight on the road above them, where Bob had parked the bus. "Then we left to go get the chainsaw and the hockey mask. After Monster took off, I left. But the plan had been for us to hide behind that rock" – he pointed – "and we were going to make a bunch of noise."

"Okay, I'm with you so far," Belle said.

"Then I was going to yell, 'Where is my arm?' Jer was going to jump out with the hockey mask and the chainsaw. He's got a broken arm, so we figured he'd look the most like Cropsy."

"Well, they'd figure it out fast enough, wouldn't they?" Clarissa said. "That it was a prank?" She looked really scared. Nat could relate.

"It doesn't look that way," Belle snapped. She tried her cell again, and when it obviously didn't work, Nat thought she was going to throw it on the ground and stomp on it, she looked so angry.

Then Dan got a funny look on his face. "We were working on our boats. They're just down at the lake."

"Show us," Belle said. She looked at Clarissa, Nat and Jenna. "Everyone, stick together. No wandering off."

Flashlights on, they walked past the tents. They continued on, reaching an embankment. Dan was in the lead.

Dan swept his flashlight over the shore as Belle, Nat, Jenna and Clarissa reached the top of the slope. All Nat saw was the shoreline.

"Where are the boats?" Belle asked, standing beside him.

Dan cleared his throat. "They're gone." He aimed his flashlight at a section of ground just below them. "We left them right there."

Nat and Jenna traded frightened looks.

"Is it possible they got unmoored in the storm?" Clarissa asked.

"They were beached." Dan looked at Belle. "If they took them..."

She spoke over him. "Why would they take your boats? Where would they go?"

"I don't know," he replied. "Maybe Jer scared them so badly they took off in our boats."

"*In the dark?*" Belle asked. She gestured for everyone to start down the embankment. Nat and Jenna hopped to. So did Dan and Clarissa. Monster bounded ahead, barking.

"If the girls took your boats, then where's Jeremiah?" Clarissa asked.

"Maybe he went to get help." He looked over at Belle, and Nat couldn't read his expression in the darkness. "There was a hole in my boat," he confessed.

Oh, no, Natalie thought. Suddenly the happy ending that had been so closely within reach was falling apart.

Belle stopped walking. She faced him squarely and shone her flashlight in his face. "A *hole*...like a hole that would make it *sink?*"

Dan gazed hard at the water, as if studying every centimetre. "Maybe. It would depend on how many people were in it. If it was Jer using my boat, going after the girls in his boat, that would probably be okay. There wouldn't be much weight in it."

But not the other way around, Nat translated. *If he has the good boat all to himself, and they're in the broken one...*

"This is all my fault!" Clarissa wailed.

"Clarissa, focus," Belle said sharply. "We need to stay calm. We need to think about what to do."

Clarissa swallowed and nodded. "Sorry."

"Were there any life jackets in the boats?" Belle asked.

He sighed. "Yes. Two in mine and one in his." He sucked in his breath. "But we didn't bring my oars. Just his."

"Maybe someone else took the boats," Jenna suggested. Her voice shook. "Do lots of kids come up here to fish?"

"Not really," Dan said, hedging.

He's hiding something, Nat thought.

"Why not?" Belle asked. "A big lake like this would have lots of fish."

He swallowed hard. "Usually. It's been quiet lately. But boating's not permitted."

"Because...?" Belle asked.

"Dead Man's Falls. They're dangerous." He pointed to the left. "They're a few kilometres down that way. The pull here is real strong. A boat without oars would

236

have a lot of trouble staying away from them."

Belle's face grew paler, if that were possible. She touched her fingertips to her forehead as if she were trying to steady herself. Nat saw that her hand was shaking. Then she lowered her arm to her side and turned to Clarissa.

"Try to call the police," she said. *"Now."*

Clarissa did as she asked, while Nat and Jenna walked to the water's edge and hoarsely yelled the names of all their bunkmates at the top of their lungs. Nat didn't care if she ruined her voice for ever. She didn't care about anything except finding her friends alive and safe.

"Chelsea!"

"Gaby!"

"Brynn!"

It went on, a 5A roll call. Their voices echoed in ghostly ripples over the fog-laden surface.

No answer. Freaking, Nat turned around to ask her counsellor for instructions on what to do next.

Belle was standing very still with her head cocked, listening to the phone. Finally she took a deep breath, flicked it shut, and raised her chin. She looked at Dan.

"Is there any chance he loaded up the boats and took the girls to the market?"

"I guess," he said, "but I doubt he'd bother doing

that in the storm. He'd just turn the boats over and leave them onshore."

Without another word, Belle jogged up and down the shoreline, scanning every centimetre with her flashlight. Nat, Jenna and Clarissa joined in. Monster raced up and down.

Out of breath, Belle planted her hands on her knees and bent over. "We're moving to Plan B," she informed them.

Plan B was to get to Dan's truck and go for help. Nat's head was spinning. The idea that her friends might have drowned...she couldn't go there. Jenna started crying. So did Nat.

"It's going to be okay," Clarissa said.

Nat wanted to lash out at her, because it might *not* be okay. Stuff like this really happened. People really did go out on dangerous lakes in leaky boats. Then other people told campfire stories about the Missing Bunk of Camp Lakeview.

They half walked, half ran through very dark, dense woods. They kept yelling for everyone. Monster barked insistently.

Jenna whispered, "You don't think they've...that the boat sank and..."

"Don't even say it," Nat pleaded. The two friends fell silent. Nat's heart beat painfully in her chest.

After what seemed like hours, Dan pushed through a narrow space between two pines, turning to help Belle through. She, in turn, helped Nat, then Jenna, then finally Clarissa.

"The truck should be just beyond these bushes," he said, stepping through dripping wet leaves.

The moonlight shone down on an empty muddy clearing.

"It's gone," Dan announced.

"No," Clarissa moaned. "Oh, no."

"So Jeremiah took them to the market," Nat said, crossing her fingers. She looked at Belle. "Right?"

"What are we going to do?" Clarissa blurted. She was getting panicky.

"Calm down, Clarissa. Try to call the police from here on your phone." Belle handed Dan's phone to him. "You too."

All three made the attempt. No one got through.

"Okay, either he drove them somewhere to get out of the rain, or he realized they were in the boats and took the truck to get help," Belle said as she put away her phone. "Or he never even saw them because they left the campsite before he got there." Wearily, she rubbed her forehead again. "Whatever the case, we need to step this up."

"I'm so sorry, Belle," Clarissa said again. "I should never have left them."

Belle just glared at her. Nat felt sorry for Clarissa, but she was grateful Belle was there. She figured everything would have turned out differently if Clarissa had gone after Chelsea, and Belle had stayed at the campfire with the rest of the bunk.

Belle's a really good counsellor, Nat realized. *We're lucky to have her. If we get out of this, I'm going to be as great a camper as I can.*

"I can lead you out to the highway," Dan said. "Maybe we can flag someone down to get us to the market."

Belle turned to Clarissa. "We should cover as many bases as possible. Clarissa, you go with Dan to the highway. Dan, tell me how to get to Dead Man's Falls. I'm taking Natalie and Jenna with me. We're going to go back along the water towards the falls and search."

"I can take them," Clarissa ventured.

"No." Belle regarded her steadily. "They're staying with me."

Nat was beyond grateful to hear that. From the look on Jenna's face, she was too.

Belle said to Clarissa and Dan, "Try to reach me on

my cell if you get a ride. At the least, check in every thirty minutes. For all we know, a call may eventually get through. But pay attention to your battery. The last thing we need is to run out of juice at a crucial moment."

Something else to worry about, Nat thought.

"I should take Monster with me," Dan said, giving the dog a pat. "He'll try to follow me, anyway, and he'll be more of a distraction than a help to you. Hopefully, a driver will let us take him with us."

"Okay." Belle clapped her hands like a coach before the big game. "Let's move."

Someone's here, the man thought, listening as he sat in the lair of the Shadow Lake Monster. He had a utility light angled over his right shoulder as he tried to clean one of the heads. Time had not been kind to them. Maybe he should just get some new ones.

Someone's sneaking around, like they used to do before I sealed up the place.

Then he had a thought: *It can't be them yet. Can it? I'm not ready.*

With an angry huff, he set down the head beside a row of rusty, dusty relays and put on his miner's helmet. The sensor board flickered, indicating that someone was wandering around inside the house. Or else it was rats again.

His eye narrowed as he flicked on the light attached to the brim of his hat. It shone down on his single eye and added a sheen to his black leather eyepatch.

Then he rose and picked up the axe.

"Who's there?" he called. "You'd better come out, or you'll be sorry."

Scowling, he limped from the room.

The Shadow Lake Monster, a huge, greenish-black creature with crocodile eyes, fangs and gills, creaked in the shadows, alone.

Up to her neck in the icy lake, Brynn felt as if her body was made of concrete. She was trying to keep her legs curled up under the boat. She was afraid of the things in the water. They were probably fish, but she couldn't stop imagining the kids in the school bus, or Randy, or Cropsy.

And she couldn't see Alex's flashlight any more. None of them could.

Brynn had never been more afraid in her entire life. She didn't know how much longer she could hold onto the boat. What if she let go and they couldn't grab her in the icy darkness? What if she *died* out here?

She fought hard not to lose control. She guessed the others were at breaking point, too. No one was talking much. From the moment they'd lost sight of Alex's flashlight, gloom had descended on them like a heavy weight.

Her heart was thudding dully in her ears. She was shuddering so hard she was getting a headache.

Then, from across the water, she heard music. Weird, creepy, spooky-ooky music.

Am I asleep? she thought. *Is this all a bad dream?*

"Guys? Do you hear that?" she asked the others.

"Hear what?" Priya asked her.

Or am I going crazy?

It was the Chamber of Horrors.

Somehow Chelsea had crashed through the roof of what appeared to be an old, abandoned funhouse. But *fun* was the wrong word. So was *abandoned*. Someone else was inside it, playing with the electricity. Every once in a while, a light would go on, or scary music would start playing, and totally freak her out.

The man lying on the table was the Frankenstein monster. The other man...well, all she could figure out was that he was being electrocuted. Both were dummies wired for chills and thrills.

Chelsea herself was *not* wired for chills and thrills. She was wired for getting out of here.

Trembling, her left ankle one continual throb of pain, she continued to stagger down a narrow, dark tunnel made of wood. It led from the room where the two dummies were arranged, and she had no idea if it was really long or if she was simply moving very slowly. It seemed to stretch for ever, and every once in a while, when she stopped to rest, she would stare into the blackness and wonder when it would end.

Now and then, lights overhead winked on and off, revealing lengths and lengths of cobwebs looping from one side of the ceiling to the other. There were so many of them swathed so low that she couldn't avoid them all, and they were sticky and thick, like candyfloss. When she tried to wipe them off her face, she got more on her hands. She used her teeth to scrape some threads off her mouth and spat as hard as she could. Then she took a step forward on her right foot, which was her good one.

A sickly green light flashed on about a metre above her head, revealing a glowing skull and crossbones mounted to the wall. The jawbone flopped open.

Chelsea jumped. Then she balled her fists and pulled her lips over her teeth to keep herself from making any noise.

"Arrr!" The jawbone snapped shut. Crazy laughter echoed in the distance.

It's just pretend.

The light went out. The laughter stopped.

Then she heard the music again. It was screechy violins and an organ. It made her scalp prickle and her spine stiffen.

It was like the funhouse was waking up. She tried not to think of all the horror movies she had watched about haunted houses. When the ghosts realized you were there, they started trying to scare you. She swore she'd never watch another one, if she could just get out of here.

Slowly, edging through the darkness, Chelsea kept going. Then another green light flashed on and a white-faced, red-mouthed clown popped out at her with its arms stretched towards her. Laughter billowed around it like fog.

It's just a statue, she reminded herself, but her heart was trying to leap from her chest.

More lights flicked on overhead. There was another clown at the end of the corridor. A green light shone directly down on it, concealing its eyes while highlighting its mouth, which was full of broken plaster teeth.

Chelsea didn't want to go past it. She looked back the way she had come. The room with the two dummies was the only other thing back there. There was no other exit between there and here. She knew; she had looked. If she wanted to get out of here, she would have to keep going forward.

She limped down the corridor until she was an arm's length from the clown, and she heard herself whimper. She was so scared. The clown was just a *thing*, just a statue, but she was still afraid of it. Summoning up every last bit of her courage, she took another step closer to its huge, grinning face.

The lights went out.

"No," she whispered. In her head, she could see the face of the clown, smiling evilly at her. She could imagine it blinking its eyes and raising its arms, getting ready to choke her.

And then she saw a light bouncing off the side of the corridor. It was very faint, as if it were shining somewhere far away.

Someone's coming, she thought. She didn't know if she was relieved or more afraid.

A voice shouted, "Is someone in here? You'd better show yourself, or you'll be sorry!" It was a man's voice. A very *angry* man's voice.

Chelsea ducked to the side of the clown statue, half expecting it to shout out, *"Here she is!"* as she bent down and peered in the direction of the light.

Then another, stronger light blossomed behind the approaching figure, revealing who had spoken.

It was a man, wearing a helmet with a light attached to it. A man with a hideous face and an eyepatch.

A man carrying an axe.

It was Cropsy!

CHAPTER FIFTEEN

I dropped the flashlight into the water because I'm getting more light-headed, Alex thought. Her forehead was beaded with sweat, and not just from the waterlogged, post-storm summer night. She was getting seriously nauseated, and she didn't know what to do. She was afraid to tell Jeremiah. He might try to turn around and head back towards their campsite — back where there was a life-saving insulin kit. But she couldn't abandon her friends.

"I see a light! It's them!" Jeremiah shouted.

Alex gazed through bleary eyes at the foggy expanse ahead of them. Sure enough, a yellow light was winking through the clumps of white.

"You guys!" Alex shouted. She stopped rowing to wave her hands. "Hey!"

Jeremiah joined in, waving, yelling!

"I see them!" Alex told him, jabbing her hands slightly to the left. "Go that way!"

They began rowing as fast as they could go.

Brynn kept swimming alongside the boat. "You guys? Seriously, I hear music."

Everyone fell silent. "I do too," Priya announced. "It sounds like circus music. What do you call those things?"

"Calliopes?" Brynn said, slowly. "Like in the musical *Carousel.*"

"Is it a radio?" Priya asked.

"What radio station plays calliope music?" Alyssa said.

"Maybe a circus is coming to town," Brynn suggested. "Do you remember if there was a circus around here last summer? Maybe that story Jordan told about the escaped lions had a grain of truth in it."

"I don't remember anything like that," Priya said.

But Brynn squinted, concentrating as more whispery, ghostlike music played through the fog.

And then she heard something wonderful. Something incredible. She heard Alex!

"Alex!" she cried. "It's Alex!"

"I hear her too!" Priya was shrieking.

"I do too!" Candace announced.

"Me four!" Alyssa croaked.

"Shine your flashlights!" Brynn said.

* * *

"Get us to Alex," Priya urged Brynn and Alyssa as the two started swimming towards Alex's boat. Alyssa was kicking as hard as she could and doing the Australian crawl with her free left hand. But she could feel the boat's momentum taking it in the other direction. She figured Alex's boat would probably drift towards theirs sooner or later, but she tried to close the distance as fast as she could anyway. She didn't want to risk moving away from them again.

Before she knew it, the guy in Alex's boat was cupping one hand around his mouth.

"I'm Jeremiah. Here's the situation. We're heading for a dangerous waterfall."

"I knew it!" Brynn croaked. When Priya and Alyssa both blinked at her in surprise, she shrugged innocently. "I didn't want to scare you guys."

"I have a rope," he said, holding up a length of rope. "Alex is tying the other end around the bench in my boat. I'm going to throw it to you, and I want each one of you to swim along it until you reach my boat. Then one of you needs to take over rowing from Alex. She doesn't feel well."

Uh-oh, Alyssa thought. *Did Alex take her insulin?*

"You mean we're leaving our boat?" Priya asked him.

"Yes," he said. "If you all crawl into my boat, it'll overload it, so I want three of you to hang onto the outside. We'll row towards land. We're actually pretty close to the opposite side of the lake."

"Oh man," Priya murmured, "this is so freaky. I can't believe this is really happening."

"We're close to land," Alyssa reminded her. "It's almost over." *For us, anyway. But what about Alex?*

"Just a little while longer," Candace said.

"I know you can do it, guys," Alex murmured.

Alyssa's ears pricked. Alex didn't sound right. Her voice was slurring.

"Okay, you two in the boat, this is up to you. Someone needs to shine a light and the other girl should try to catch the rope," Brynn said. "But watch it. Don't tip the boat over!"

"Candace, you man the flashlight," Priya said. "I'll try to catch the rope."

Candace gripped the flashlight with both hands.

"Ready."

"Priya, just pretend it's a basketball," Alyssa urged her.

"I'm playing horse with Jordan," she announced. "And this court is mine!"

"Go Priya, go Priya," Alyssa cheered.

On the other side of the boat, Brynn took up the cheer. "Go, Priya, go Priya." Candace joined in too, squawking away.

"Okay, I'm going to throw it to you," Jeremiah said. "I'm a little off-balance because of my arm."

"Ready!" Priya croaked at the guy. "Bring it on!"

Jeremiah stood up and spread his legs wide apart. He held the rope up over his head like a cowboy. Alyssa stopped swimming and extended her free hand into the air. She was on the left side of the boat, furthest away from him, but she would be ready just in case.

"Here it comes!" he yelled.

Priya's arms jutted into the air.

Alyssa could just make out the wavy line in the glow of the flashlight before a cry of disappointment rose up from inside the boat. Then she heard a light splash on the opposite side.

"Didn't get it!" Priya rasped. "Try again!"

"Okay," he said.

"Wait," Alyssa said. "Brynn and I should hold flashlights so Candace and Priya can both try to catch the rope."

"That's a great idea," Brynn agreed. "Let's try it."

Alex's boat glided towards theirs as Candace and Priya lowered a flashlight each to Brynn and Alyssa. Alyssa shined hers at Alex's boat. "Alex, are you okay?"

"I'm pretty good," Alex said. But she didn't sound pretty good. She sounded terrible.

Jeremiah was working to keep his balance. He held the rope over his head again.

"Here it comes!"

Alyssa focused her flashlight just above his head. She saw it fly out of his hands. Here it came...

"Yes!" Priya squeaked as Candace jumped up and seized the rope. "We've got it!"

The boat rocked back and forth, back and forth. Then her side of the boat flew way up in the air. Alyssa dangled from it for a heart-stopping second as the boat went up and over, crashing into the water and ramming her hard beneath the icy waters of Shadow Lake.

Alyssa plummeted beneath the surface. The shock of the cold water made her eyelids flutter, and she saw nothing but icy blackness. She had dropped her flashlight when the boat had capsized.

She fought her way to the surface, gasping for air.

"Brynn! Candace! Priya!" she shouted.

"I'm good!" Brynn managed. "Candace! Priya! Lyss, I think they're trapped under the boat!"

"No! I'm here!" Priya said, coughing hard.

"Candace! Answer me! Where are you?" Alyssa yelled. "Help us!" she screamed at Jeremiah.

"Candace!" everyone shouted.

Jeremiah leaped into the water and started one-armed swimming for them.

Alyssa took a breath, held onto the side of the overturned boat, and ducked beneath the surface. She shut her eyes tightly and reached into the upside-down boat, searching for Candace. Her heart pounded in her ears as she darted her arm left, right, centre.

She's not in here, Alyssa thought. She jabbed her hand downwards, and then she prepared to surface to get another breath of air.

Then fingers reached wildly for her. *Candace!* Alyssa wrapped her hand around the fingers and tried to pull her up. But Candace was pulling her under. She was about to lose her grip on the boat. And she was running out of air.

Then the fingers loosened.

And then...they went away.

No! Alyssa thought, reaching further, feeling into the blackness more desperately.

Nothing.

She breached above the waterline, gasping so hard she couldn't talk.

"There she is!" Alex cried from the other boat.

Jeremiah crashed to the surface with Candace in his arm. She was coughing hard. Alyssa knew that was a good sign. That meant her lungs were clearing.

"Candace, are you all right?" Brynn cried.

"Yes." She coughed some more. "I'm fine." Then she began to cry.

"The rope, get the rope," Alex yelled. "Take Candace to the other boat."

"Here it is! I've got it!" Brynn said. She lifted it over her head for all to see.

"Hold it tight," Jeremiah said. "I'll take Candace over and then I'll come back and hold it for the rest of you." Then he added, "Alex is having some trouble. Do any of you have any candy?"

"Um, I do," Candace said. "I wore pyjama shorts with pockets so I could bring some candy. And my good-luck worry doll. I have a packet of Skittles and some sour apple jawbreakers. But they're probably soaked."

"I don't think Alex will care," he said. "You go first, hand over hand. It's better if you don't try to swim. You guys are cold and tired and you can probably feel the pull of the water towards the falls. When you reach my boat, give the Skittles to Alex."

"Got it."

Everybody watched Candace manoeuvre across the rope. When she reached Jeremiah's boat, they all cheered. She gave Alex the Skittles, and Alex ate them one right after another, quickly devouring the package.

Priya went next, then Brynn, and finally Alyssa. They took up their positions alongside the boat, then Jeremiah swam back and awkwardly flopped inside as Alex helped him. When he sat down on the bench, she gave him a quick hug and he smiled at her as she moved off the bench. Candace took her place.

"I'm a really good rower." She lifted her chin.

No one argued.

Jeremiah and Candace took up the oars and began to row. Brynn, Priya and Alyssa held on tight. Alyssa swept Jeremiah's flashlight over the lake.

The beam passed over dark shapes jutting into the sky. They were trees. She moved the beam lower to see a bank, and further down, the shoreline.

"Land," she said in a hushed whisper. "We're almost there."

The girls cheered. Jeremiah's smile grew. He and Candace kept rowing, and Alyssa found comfort in the rhythm of the oars as they dipped into the water.

Then Alyssa heard the weird, creepy music again. It was drifting over the water like fog.

Jeremiah tilted his head. "Do you guys hear music?"

"Yes," Alyssa told him. "Do you know what it is?"

"I think I do," he said, gazing at her, "and it's totally freaking me out."

Alyssa was afraid to ask, but she had to.

"Why?"

"Because it goes with the story of Cropsy that *I* heard. It's different from the one your friend told you guys, but it's just as scary."

"*No*," Brynn wailed. "Not another Cropsy story!"

"Maybe you should tell it. It might help us find Chelsea," Alyssa said.

"For all we know, she's been found," Brynn said. "*Please*, no more scary stories!"

"I think we have to hear it," Alex insisted.

"We have to hear it," Candace agreed.

"When we get to land, I'll tell it," Jeremiah promised.

"*If* we get to land," Brynn muttered.

"We should just stop," Gaby told Tori as the truck inched along. "We can't see where we're going."

"Sorry," Tori said, staring into the fog. She was so bummed. The rain had cleared the fog away, and they'd been good to go. But then they had dipped down into a valley, and a new fog bank had drifted over the road, almost as if it were trying to keep them from seeing where they were going.

"What if a car comes from the other direction?" Gaby said. "It might hit us."

"We need to get help for the bunk," Tori argued.

"We're not going to be able to get help if we get into an accident," Gaby argued back. "Seriously, Tori, you need to pull over."

"Guys?" Valerie said. "Look."

In the fog ahead of their headlights, three or four dark shapes shifted and moved. They looked as though they were floating about a metre off the ground.

"Look out!" Gaby cried. She grabbed the wheel and turned it to the right.

"Gaby, no!" Tori shouted.

The truck turned. They were going so slowly that there was no danger of losing control of the steering. But the fog was so thick that there was every danger of running into something they couldn't see.

Sure enough, the truck hit something hard and jerked to a stop.

Tori gunned the engine. It wouldn't go. Grunting, she put the truck in reverse. It backed up...and then stopped again.

"We're stuck," she said.

"We're *trapped*," Valerie replied.

Then something bumped against Tori's door.

* * *

"Land, sweet land," Priya crooned, kneeling down and pretending to kiss the mud while Jeremiah and Candace made sure the little fishing boat was securely pulled up on the shore.

"Amen," Brynn said, kneeling down beside her.

Alex and Alyssa joined them, and they gave each other a group hug. Then Candace trotted over, making it five bunkmates who had worked together to survive the ordeal.

As they hugged, the eerie calliope music wafted through the muggy night. They all heard it, raising their heads and listening.

"It's louder now," Alex pointed out. She looked at Jeremiah. "About that story. You said you'd tell it once we hit land."

The girls looked at him expectantly. He took a deep breath and began.

"Okay. Here goes. It's been said that in the 1950s, a man named Elias Croppersly built an amusement park in the hills of Shadow Lake. It was like a carnival, with a few rides, some games and a freak show. The big attraction was the Chamber of Horrors. There were all kinds of terrifying scenes of murder and death, and some of it was so gory that the locals complained. But Croppersly just made it gorier.

"He had a real guillotine shipped over from France.

The guillotine was used for executions during the French Revolution in the 1700s. A razor-sharp blade would be raised high into the air. Then a condemned prisoner was tied down and the razor-sharp blade would descend...and slice off his head!

"Kids loved to sneak into the amusement park after hours. The boys would throw rocks at the lights and steal props. Croppersly warned them all that if they kept it up, they'd pay...and pay dearly. That just encouraged them to do it more.

"One night, two brothers snuck into the Chamber of Horrors. The older one was named Randy, and Chris was four years younger. Elias Croppersly heard them and came after them with a gun! He chased them into the guillotine room.

"'I'm sick and tired of you kids!' he shouted at them. 'I warned you!' He aimed the gun at Chris and told Randy to lie down on the guillotine. He strapped him in. Randy started struggling and screaming, and Chris begged for his brother's life, but Croppersly was determined.

"Then he turned on the Chamber of Horrors soundtrack, and laughed as the awful music drowned out Chris and Randy's shrieks of terror.

"As Chris looked on helplessly, the blade came down! And Randy's head was chopped clear off his body!

Blood from his neck sprayed everywhere. Then his head plopped like a gooshy watermelon into a basket.

"Croppersly unstrapped his bleeding corpse. It fell to the floor, blood pooling around the legs of the guillotine. Croppersly and Chris slipped in it as Croppersly grabbed Randy's fainting brother and flung him onto the guillotine. Chris was in shock and he didn't fight Croppersly, who still had the gun, as he rebuckled the straps, soaked with Randy's blood.

"Then Croppersly raised the blade and got ready to let it go!

"But just as he reached for the rope to release the blade, Randy's headless body rose from the floor of the Chamber of Horrors. It staggered over to Croppersly and threw its arms around him. Croppersly shot his gun, but the bullets did nothing to stop the corpse. It stretched the evil man's arm beneath the path of the guillotine blade and unstrapped Chris!

"Chris rolled free just as the blade plummeted, cutting off Croppersly's arm at the shoulder. Croppersly screamed as blood gushed from his arm.

"Then Randy's body collapsed.

"And from inside the basket, his head whispered, *'Run, Chris, run!'*

"The amusement park was closed the next day, for ever...and the forest reclaimed the land. Legend has it that Croppersly still roams the woods, searching for the boy who escaped the guillotine, which took his own arm instead."

The music had grown much louder by the time Jeremiah finished his tale of terror. The girls looked at one another. For a moment, no one spoke.

"Okay, I don't like that story, either," Brynn declared. Training her flashlight in his direction, she narrowed her eyes at Jeremiah. "Is this part of your plan to scare us? Is your friend hiding in the woods and playing music on a boom box? Because that music sounds very close."

"Yeah," Candace said. "Are you still pranking us?"

"No. I swear." Jeremiah held up his hand. "There's absolutely no way." He hesitated. "I have never heard that music before. Some friends of mine said they heard it when we were little kids, but I never did. Until now."

"Do you think this has something to do with Chelsea?" Alex asked.

"Chelsea's missing, and Croppersly's music is playing...you don't think he would cut off her head?" Brynn covered her mouth with her hands and let out a squeak.

"I've never found the amusement park," Jeremiah

said. "No one has. And we've looked. But we can follow the music."

"We can find a way out of here and call the police," Brynn interjected.

Jeremiah took a breath. "The quickest way out of here is to go back across the lake. The hike out would take hours any other way."

The music swelled. Everyone looked at one another.

"I think at least two of us should row back across," Priya suggested. "Maybe Belle and the others are back at the campsite. Are you too tired, Jeremiah?"

"No, but..." He turned his head. "Oh, no! Look!"

The boat was gone.

"No!" Brynn cried. She leaped to her feet and raced to the water. Priya joined her and they dashed in up to their ankles, shining their flashlights. Alyssa joined them, followed by Candace.

Their slumped shoulders told the story. The boat was gone.

Candace was the first to return. She was crying. "Didn't I do a good job of pulling it up onshore?"

"You did fine," Jeremiah said. "*I'm* the one who messed up."

"Yeah, to make your prank work better," Priya said.

"Yeah." Candace wiped her eyes. "How convenient."

"I swear that's not it." Jeremiah shook his head. "With your friend Alex sick? No way."

Alex shifted. "I do need my insulin," she admitted. "I should probably go to hospital once...this is over."

"So, all that's left is to follow the music," Priya said.

"It's like we're being forced into the clutches of Cropsy." Brynn clutched her hands beneath her chin.

"Oh, don't be so dramatic," Priya said.

"Dramatic? Hello? We just nearly drowned!" Brynn cried. "I'd say a little drama is in order!"

Alex privately agreed with Brynn. But she said aloud, "We should go check it out. Just in case. Don't forget, we're Bunk 5A and we are *solid*!"

"Woo-hoo!" Candace cried. "Solid!"

"You guys are doing great," Belle said as she, Natalie and Jenna turned back from the headwaters of Dead Man's Falls. There was no evidence of the two dinghies, and no way to tell if they had gone over the falls or not. But Belle just moved on to Plan C. She stayed amazingly calm, and she kept Jenna and Natalie calm too.

She rocks, Jenna thought. *She's the best counsellor I've ever had.*

Now they were following the creepy music that

echoed off the trees. Jenna stuck close to Natalie, who was trembling as hard as she was.

"Belle will keep us safe," Jenna told her.

"I know," Natalie replied.

They walked a while longer. Belle had amazing stamina.

"I keep hearing it, but I can't figure out where it is," Jenna said as the three stopped to catch their breaths. "It's almost like it's...*under* us."

"I know," Belle said, sweeping the ground with her flashlight beam. "I can't figure it out."

Inside the Chamber of Horrors, the eerie music shut off as Cropsy moved closer. He had a limp, too, and as he walked towards Chelsea, his light bobbed. Soon it would shine on Chelsea and then...oh, help, would he cut off her head?

She was shaking so badly, she didn't know if she'd be able to move. She didn't know what to do. She darted her gaze left and right, looking for inspiration.

"I know you're in there," the man said in a loud voice. "Come out now. This is your last chance."

Then his flashlight beam hit Chelsea square in the eyes.

* * *

Inside the cab of the truck, Tori, Valerie and Gaby held onto one another as more *things* bumped against the doors in the thick fog. Tori honked the horn again, but it didn't seem to faze whatever was attacking them. She gunned the engine and floored the gas pedal, but the tyres spun. Whatever had captured them, it still had them.

"What is it? What's out there?" Valerie shrieked.

Wham! Something bumped harder against the truck.

"Go away!" Tori laid on the horn.

Chelsea let out a squeak that even she couldn't hear as she leaped up and covered her eyes against the flashlight.

As she turned to get away, she stepped down hard on her bad foot. Pain shot from her ankle up through her leg and she started to fall. Her hand shot out, grabbing onto the clown statue. A piece of it broke off in her hand as she fell down.

"Hey!" Cropsy shouted.

With his axe raised over his head, he started towards her.

Chelsea looked from him to the piece of the clown statue in her hand. It was the clown's arm, broken off at the shoulder, just like Cropsy's.

She scrambled backwards, stretching out her leg and trying to crab-walk with one foot and two arms. But she couldn't do it. She was too clumsy, tired and scared.

"Stop right there! Stop!" the man yelled at her. "Don't move!"

She flung herself backwards. The floor behind her tilted downwards at a steep angle and she fell onto her back. Then she started to slide head first down what felt to be a slick metal slide.

She screamed all the way down. Really screamed, her terror pushing her voice past her hoarseness.

"I hear her!" Nat yelled. "She's close!" She whirled in a circle, cupping her hands and bellowing, "Chelsea!"

"She's underneath us," Belle yelled, pointing her flashlight. "She's fallen into a mine or something." She kept her flashlight pointed downwards.

Then she shouted, "Look!"

In the middle of the forest ground, there was a jagged hole. It was barely big enough for someone to fall through.

Belle dropped to her knees. "Chelsea?"

* * *

267

As they tromped through the woods, Alex heard Chelsea screaming and her heart skipped beats.

"Come on!" Brynn yelled, taking off. Alyssa and Priya followed after her.

Dizzy and nauseated again, Alex stopped walking.

"I'm in trouble," she told Jeremiah.

Without a word, Jeremiah scooped Alex up in his one good arm, flung her over his shoulder, and jogged toward the screams.

They all ran.

CHAPTER SIXTEEN

Screaming, Chelsea hurtled down the slide through the darkness. Then she sailed into the air and landed back first on another dusty mattress.

Dazed, she panted for a few seconds. Then she made herself sit up. She grabbed onto the end of the slide and painfully got to her feet. Her ankle burned.

She had lost the clown arm. She had no weapons.

She turned around and started limping with her arms outstretched. There was no litter on the ground. It smelled better too.

She kept going, with no clue what to do next. She didn't know how long she could keep limping on her foot. She wished she had something to use as a crutch or a walking stick. She could use it to whack Cropsy if he came after her again.

A dim light played over her surroundings. She stopped.

Should she go towards it, or stay away? She didn't know what to do.

Footsteps pounded overhead. He was looking for her!

She limped forwards. As the light grew stronger, she saw an entrance to a room. There was a sign over it that read, THE LAIR OF THE SHADOW LAKE MONSTER.

Chelsea moved to the side of the entrance and peered in. She grabbed the wall to hold herself up as her knees buckled.

A wooden table littered with tools sat to one side. There was a light in a metal cylinder attached to a ladder. The light shone on...*heads*! There were three of them, one facing her, with eyes that were all white, its mouth frozen in a scream.

It's a prop, she told herself, but it looked too real. She'd seen a lot of horror movies where the crazy killer had hidden the real bodies among the fake ones.

And he came after me with an axe!

Behind the table, a huge dark green figure stood about two metres tall. It had eyes like an alligator, and its finned arms stretched menacingly towards Chelsea. It looked like a cross between a man and a fish, with bulgy eyes and fleshy lips with fangs. Fins stuck out from the sides of its bald head, and its arms and feet ended in flippers.

"Game's over," Cropsy said.

Chelsea whirled around.

He was standing in his miner's hat, his axe slung over his shoulder. She could see nothing else in the yellow glare of his flashlight.

Help me.

Tears streaming down her face, she ducked into the room, immediately realizing her mistake. Now she was trapped. She limped as fast as she could towards the table of tools...and the heads...searching for something to hit him with. There! A big wrench!

She had to reach in front of one of the heads to grab it, but she made herself do it. Then she turned around and raised it up. She wouldn't go down without a fight. She thought of her parents, and her sister, and all her bunkmates.

Goodbye, she said to them all, even Natalie and Jenna, who had been so mean to her.

She trembled all over as she shook the wrench at him.

"Don't you come near me!"

He took another step towards her.

"You are in such big trouble."

"Chelsea!" It was Belle! Belle was calling her name!

He took another step towards her.

"Belle! Help! Help me!" Chelsea cried, but she had

finally pushed her voice past its limits. The words came out in a hoarse whisper. But she didn't give up.

"It's Cropsy! Call the police!" she rasped.

"I've already called the police," Cropsy said. "They're on their way."

CHAPTER SEVENTEEN

"Chelsea!" Belle yelled again. "Can you hear us?"

Nat cried out, "Belle! Jenna! Look!"

About ten metres past the hole, there was a slope. Belle and Jenna came up behind Nat.

"Maybe we can get to Chelsea that way," Nat said.

"Okay, follow me," Belle said, taking the lead, "but not too close."

Nat sandwiched herself between Jenna and Belle. They walked-ran down the incline until they came to a thick wall of trees. Belle handed the flashlight to Nat, reached up, grabbed hold of one of the branches as if she were going to do a chin-up, and pulled down hard.

"Here, we'll help," Jenna said. She came up beside Belle, who wasn't much taller than she was, and started yanking on the same branch.

It broke and crashed to the ground.

"Hey, I see something," Nat said. She aimed her

flashlight through the space they had made.

It was the word DANGER written in black.

Belle broke off another branch. Jenna helped. Then Belle doubled up and rammed herself against the danger sign.

There was a cracking sound. She did it again. Another cracking sound.

"Please," she said to Nat, reaching for the flashlight. She slammed the end of it against the wood, and a piece broke off. She had a peephole now, and she peered into it.

"Oh no," she said. Then she raised her voice and shouted, "Chelsea! We're coming!"

"Come on, girls," she said to Jenna and Nat. "Hurry!"

With Alex over Jeremiah's shoulder, the six raced towards the screams. In the lead, Priya pushed through a curtain of pine branches to see —

"It's true!" Priya cried.

"What?" Brynn rammed into her from behind. "What do you see?"

A half-rotted wooden fence, large pieces missing, bore the words CROP 'S AMUS ME TS in faded black paint. It was surrounded with images — a vampire, a clown, balloons and a cone of candyfloss.

Lower down were several signs, tacked one on top of another: CONDEMNED. NO ENTRY. DANGER. TRESPASSERS WILL BE PROSECUTED.

"Alyssa, the flashlight," Priya said.

Priya pushed her head through the fence and shone the light over the silhouette of a small broken-down roller coaster and a merry-go-round. Further back, there was a building shaped like a big skull. Its mouth was a set of large double doors standing half-open. She could just make out the sign, CHAMBER OF HORRORS.

"Jeremiah's story is true!" Priya yelled. "Come on, help me break down this fence!"

"Wait. *You* called the police?" Chelsea said.

"Of course I did. You're trespassing." The man set down his axe. "I should have figured someone would hear the music."

Just then, there was a tremendous racket behind him. He turned around.

And there was Belle!

No questions asked, Belle charged right at the man. She was a total warrior! She tackled him, throwing her arms around him and pushing him backwards onto the floor.

275

"Ai-ya!" she bellowed. Then she rested her sneaker on his windpipe, her back straight, and her hands flat and extended in a karate-type stance.

Jenna appeared next, followed by Natalie, both still in their pyjamas.

"Chelsea, are you all right?" Belle shouted.

Chelsea started to cry again, but she nodded. Then she sank to the floor.

"Chelsea, oh, Chelsea!" Natalie threw her arms around her and hugged her tightly.

Jenna ran over to where the man lay flat on his back and shone her flashlight on him and Belle.

"I've called the State Troopers!" the man gurgled. "They're on their way."

"What?" Belle remained in position.

"You'll all be arrested for trespassing," he continued. "And attacking me!"

"Who are you?" Belle asked him.

"I'm Jamieson Cropwell. Who are you?"

"One, two, three!" Priya shouted.

The group pushed on the fence. Jeremiah had settled Alex on the ground, propped against a pine tree. He, Priya, Alyssa, Brynn and Candace nearly had it all the way down.

Priya looked through the slats.

And then she saw Natalie and Jenna emerging from the mouth of the skull building!

"Natalie!" Priya shrieked, but her voice was gone. "Alyssa," she whispered, "yell!"

Alyssa shouted, "Natalie!"

Natalie heard Alyssa and raced towards the fence. She was yelling and waving her hands.

"You guys! Oh, you guys!" she croaked. She gripped her hands around one of the boards and yanked. "We found Chelsea!"

"Is she okay?" Alyssa asked.

"Her ankle's hurt. Belle thinks it's just a sprain."

"Alex needs her insulin," Alyssa said.

"I'll go tell Belle, okay? Mr. Cropwell called the State Troopers. Maybe they can bring some. I'll go get Belle!"

Natalie turned and trotted back to the skull building.

Alyssa and Priya looked at each other, and then at Jeremiah. "Mr. Cropwell?" Alyssa said slowly.

Gaby, Tori and Valerie jumped and clung to one another. It had been half an hour since something had banged on the truck. Tori had turned off the headlights to conserve the truck's battery, but the girls were still afraid to get out. The fog was gone, and they'd been hoping that their monsters had left with it.

Then something hit the truck door!

"This is the Pennsylvania State Troopers. Open your door," said an amplified voice.

Something hit the door again.

Only it wasn't hitting, it was *knocking*.

Then a bright light shone in their eyes. Tori jerked and pushed against Valerie.

"Open your door," said the voice again.

Squinting, Tori unrolled the window with the hand crank just a tiny bit.

"Who are you?" she called out.

"We're State Troopers, miss," said a woman's voice. "Are you part of the missing bunk from Camp Lakeview?"

"Yes!" Valerie, Tori and Gaby yelled in unison.

Tori popped open her door and climbed down gratefully as the trooper gave her a hand. Then she jumped back in as something white bobbed towards them.

"It's okay. It's just a sheep," the trooper said, laughing.

What?

"Baaa," said the sheep.

"Hold on." Tori reached into the truck and flicked on the headlights.

A dozen sheep were milling in front of the high beams.

"Our attackers!" Tori told the others.

Gaby and Valerie started laughing.

Priya, Alyssa, Natalie, Jenna, Brynn and Jeremiah accompanied Mr. Cropwell on a quick tour of the Chamber of Horrors, while Belle used Mr. Cropwell's landline phone. First she made sure the closest hospital had some insulin, and then she called Dr. Steve. He and Nurse Helen would meet the group there.

Chelsea's ankle was too sore for any more adventures.

"Besides," she said, "I've seen more than enough."

Alex was sad, though. She wasn't feeling up to going exploring. Mr. Cropwell told her he would take her on a tour another time.

"I built this place in 1953," he said, ushering them into a room with a man in an electric chair and a body wrapped in bandages. "Hmm. Water damage." He looked up. "This must be where your friend fell through the roof." He pointed to the mattress. "I was getting rid of that. Lucky thing I got tired and left it there."

"Why is everything all ruined like this?" Brynn asked. Once you got used to looking at Mr. Cropwell's face, it wasn't so bad. But Brynn could tell he was very embarrassed by his appearance. He kept ducking his head and he muttered a lot.

"Couldn't make a go of it," he said. "Not enough customers." He looked back down and muttered, "I got so mad one night, I carted out a whole bunch of dummies and threw them in the lake."

He pointed his hand towards the west. "I used to live in a little cabin on the other side of the lake. Stored lots of the Chamber of Horrors props in my basement. But things...happened. My wife died, and I had a bad accident." He gestured to his eyepatch and sighed. "This park was her dream. And when she died, I guess it died, too. I kept it hidden for years. In the early days, people remembered and they would sneak in." He pointed to the mattress. "Sometimes people even camped here. I had to shoo them away."

"I've looked for Croppersly's Chamber of Horrors ever since I was a little boy," Jeremiah said. "I even Googled it."

"You had my name wrong," Mr. Cropwell pointed out.

Jeremiah nodded, then grinned. "Well, it's a dream come true to finally find it. It was the music," he added.

"Yes. Why did you play the music?" Brynn asked Mr. Cropwell. "That's how we found you."

"I started the utilities again so I could clean the place up," he said. "Some people are thinking of putting in a playland – mini-golf, bumper cars – and reopening the Chamber of Horrors."

He looked at the ground again. "They tried to buy it a few years ago, but I held out for too much money. So this time, I thought I'd clean it up before they got here. Then maybe they'd raise their offer a little." He sighed. "But there's so much to do, and they said they'd be in touch before the end of summer."

"Maybe we can help you," Brynn said. The others nodded excitedly.

"Well, that'd be nice, but you're here to go to camp," he said.

"We'll ask," Priya announced.

"I can help for sure," Jeremiah told Mr. Cropwell. "And Dan, too."

"We could write an article on it for *The Acorn*!" Priya cried. "In fact, don't you think it should be some kind of historical site?"

He laughed, and it was a funny thing, but when he laughed, his scars didn't show.

"I don't know about that, but I have a nice scrapbook about the place."

"Oooh, can we see it?"

"Next time," Belle said from the doorway. She looked

281

at Mr. Cropwell. "The State Troopers are here."

"I'll talk to them," Mr. Cropwell said. He limped out of the room.

Belle said to the others, "Dan and Clarissa got a ride. They called the troopers too. They picked up Gaby, Valerie and Tori. They're fine."

The nightmare was really, truly over. Dr. Steve, Nurse Helen and Tashya met Belle, Alex and Chelsea at the hospital. Mr. Cropwell drove them there, then went back to ferry the others over from the ruins of his amusement park. Chelsea had a sprained ankle, and the doctor fitted her with one of those weird boot-shoes and told her to stay off it. Gaby, Valerie and Tori stayed at the trooper base.

As for Alex...

"She's good," the doctor said as he read the results of the tests he had run on her. "You guys did all the right things," he told the girls.

Candace beamed with pride.

After making absolutely sure that all his campers were in relatively good shape, Dr. Steve listened to the entire story and explained that he would have to contact all their parents to let them know what had happened.

"Some of your parents may be unhappy and may

want to take you out of camp," he said, preparing them for the worst.

It *would* be the worst, Candace realized. Sure, she had been scared – make that totally terrified – but the whole bunk had worked together and taken care of one another. She had felt needed, and important.

In fact, she felt pretty good.

The group took the bus back to the campsite to retrieve the bunk's personal belongings. Dr. Steve told them that someone else would come out in the daylight to take down the tents and collect the rest of the gear.

Before they left, the eleven bunkmates walked to the edge of the campsite and gazed down at Shadow Lake. Jeremiah and Dan were there too. The troopers were going to take them in for questioning. Candace wondered if they were in trouble. They hadn't shown good judgement, but they had pitched in to help when the bunk needed them.

"Well, some of your story was true," Alex said to Jeremiah. "There was an amusement park. Mr. 'Cropsy' Cropwell's amusement park." She emphasized his name. "But no kid got his arm cut off. There wasn't even a guillotine."

"I can't believe we never found that place before," Jeremiah said. "I grew up here. We searched every millimetre of this lake."

"Maybe tonight was a special, *spooooky* night when you were meant to find it," Valerie said, making her eyes wide and scary.

"Please don't," Gaby said, huffing. "It was the music. We all heard it."

"Mr. Cropwell's got some cool old stories about the history of Shadow Lake," Priya said. "I'm going to write them down. Maybe we can run them in *The Acorn*. I have newspaper for one of my electives."

"No more scary stories!" Brynn cried.

"Bunk 5A, we need to go," Dr. Steve told them, standing by the door of the bus.

"Well, his plan worked," Natalie said. "We have bonded. High five, 5A!"

The girls all laughed and crowded in, slapping hands together.

"Last one on the bus..." Gaby began, then trailed off. She smiled and put her arm around Chelsea's waist. "...has a sprained ankle!"

Bunk 5A had never looked so wonderful. Unfurling her sleeping bag with a practised hand, Priya fell into bed. So did everyone else.

"I'm too excited to sleep," Brynn announced.

"Me too," Natalie said.

"Me three," Candace said.

"Me four," said Chelsea.

"Girls, please, let's not get to eleven," Belle said.

And amazingly enough, they all did fall asleep.

The girls were excused from flag-raising and breakfast. But word had gotten around about their harrowing adventure, and a lot of their friends came to see them while they were still in their pyjamas. Belle allowed them in, and Jordan went straight to Brynn. Butterflies started dancing in her stomach. She would finally find out why he had wanted to talk to her.

He and Brynn sat cross-legged on the floor. He studied her face. "Wow, I can't believe what happened."

"I can't, either," Brynn replied, with a quirky half-grin. "And I was there."

Jordan shook his head. "Well, I'm really glad you're okay." He paused. "You know, I wanted to talk to you about something." He dropped his gaze to his hands.

This cannot be good, she thought. *Then again, if I survived Shadow Lake, I can survive whatever he wants to tell me.*

He looked back up at her. "I just...wanted to make sure we were okay. I saw you and...you look different from even the last time I saw you. More...grown up.

And I..." He took a breath. "I wasn't sure if you still wanted to have a...to be..."

Her heart sang. Her grin spread across her face as she said, "Do you want to go the social together? Like a date?"

He blinked rapidly. "Sure. Do you?" Then he laughed. "Well, I guess you do, if you asked." His cheeks turned pink. "Cool!"

Priya came over to Clarissa's bed. Chelsea had been moved there to make it easier on her ankle, and it was piled with presents, flowers and get-well cards. And a whole ginormous stash of candy and cupcakes from Jenna. There would definitely be no more fights about who had a top bunk.

Not that Priya thought there would be any more fights. Their bunk had become too tight for that stuff. And Priya wanted to make sure there wasn't anything else to get in the way of having a fun, cool summer. So she asked Chelsea to have a talk with her.

"About Spence," Priya said, taking a deep breath. She looked at Chelsea. "I think he likes you the best."

Chelsea's face went red. "I don't care." When Priya grinned at her, she turned even redder. "Seriously."

"Well, I've decided I don't want to have a camp

boyfriend," Priya insisted. "I don't want a guy to come between me and my bunkmate."

"Then I won't, either," Chelsea said firmly. She held up her hand. "Spence is neutral territory."

Priya laughed and high-fived her. "Okay!"

"5A rocks!" Chelsea said.

Alex looked over. "Say what?"

"5A rocks!" Priya yelled.

Everyone else took up the chant – Natalie, Jenna, Alyssa, Tori, Gaby, Valerie, Candace and Brynn – yelling, "5A rocks! 5A rocks!"

"We totally do!" Priya shouted.

EPILOGUE

...so, Grace, that's the story of Cropsy. Just a lonely old man whose dream didn't quite come true.

We solved a few more mysteries. Jer and Dan confessed to tearing down the Camp Lakeview sign and spray-painting it, as a prank. And Tori thinks Monster the dog was the panting thing that poked at her in the fog. Then when he started howling, her imagination got the best of her and she thought he was howling for his arm!

I guess Jer's plan to get Clarissa's attention worked because Clarissa's been talking about him a lot. But she's been pretty serious and strict lately. I think Dr. Steve came down pretty hard on her for leaving campers alone when we went to look for Belle and Chelsea.

Speaking of Chelsea...we have voted her Queen of the Bunk. Truth! We all realized that we didn't even give her or Gaby a chance and everyone is sorry for being so mean. We have totally hit reset. I'm making Chelsea a beaded necklace like those ones we made my first summer, and Brynn is coaching Gaby for her audition as Sarah Brown in <u>Guys and Dolls.</u> No more spooky <u>The Legend of Sleepy Hollow</u> for us!

We've been back for three whole days, and so far no one has gone home. I guess all our parents understand that what happened was a one-time thing, and they trust Dr. Steve and Belle to take care of us. And everyone is safe and sound, so that counts for something.

Turns out that we were wrong about Belle. She's not a vampire — she just doesn't tan! <u>And</u> she has a black belt in tae kwon do!

I'm sitting out on our porch, watching the sun go down, and I still have a question: <u>what was holding my hand in the fog?</u>

At first I didn't even want to think about it ever again. But you know, the thing is, I was really scared out there...and whatever it was, it gave me a warm, friendly squeeze, like it was trying to comfort me. So if there is a ghost, I think it's a nice one. Like Casper.

Hey! Chelsea just informed me that our entire division is going to have a singdown! And no one but 5A knows that Chelsea knows every single pop hit written in the 1970s! With Chelsea up for 70s hits and Brynn as our secret weapon for Broadway musicals, we are totally going to win! The other bunks are <u>in terrible danger</u> of losing.

I can't believe I just wrote that!

Anyway, gotta go. I miss you! Can't wait to see you!

XOXO,
Nat

Turn the page for a sneak
preview of more

SUMMER CAMP
SECRETS

REALITY BITES

CHAPTER ONE

"This is exactly what I needed," Chelsea said suddenly as she and the rest of bunk 5A floated lazily on inflatable rings during free swim. Gaby glanced over at her warily, not sure she wanted to hear the rest. "Peace, quiet and some nice hot rays to soak up. I mean, after everything I went through on our camping trip." Chelsea glanced up to make sure her bunkmates were listening, and Gaby could see that she was trying to look upset. "With Cropsy, and being chased...I was *so* scared, guys."

"We know," Val replied.

"I mean...waking up in an abandoned amusement park? Getting chased by some stranger?"

Tori nodded. "It must have been tough."

"It was, like, horror movie material." Chelsea shuddered.

Gaby looked away. She was annoyed. For almost a week now, Chelsea had been regaling them with tales of her horrible nightmares and flashbacks — all results of a scary time Chelsea had had on their campout, when she got lost and ended up in an abandoned amusement park tended by someone who was rumoured to be a maniac. And Gaby knew it had to have been pretty scary for Chelsea. But she'd come out of it *fine* — the guy, Cropsy, had turned out to be harmless, and Chelsea was safely returned to her bunkmates. *Is she ever going to get over it?* she wondered. For the past two years at camp, Gaby and Chelsea had gotten along okay — they had their share of arguments, but underneath it all they had an understanding. This year, though, they'd had a huge fight at the beginning of camp — and they still hadn't gotten over it. Gaby and Chelsea had barely spoken since the first day.

But now Gaby's bunkmates were making little sympathetic pouts and noises. "It must have been really hard," Brynn cooed. "I mean, we all know Cropsy turned out to be harmless. But still, getting lost in the woods by yourself...and then getting chased..."

"It's really scary," Priya agreed.

Chelsea stopped shuddering, and Gaby watched her try to hide a secret little smile as she tossed her head and leaned back against her ring. "Thanks, guys. I just, you know — it's still hard for me."

Gaby groaned inwardly. To make matters worse, she

knew that Chelsea was lying about all the nightmares and flashbacks. She'd seen Chelsea sleeping soundly one night when she claimed she hadn't gotten a wink of sleep because her flashbacks were so bad. And just like now, she'd catch a satisfied expression cross Chelsea's face each time she was supposedly freaking out about this or that – because she'd gotten what she wanted from her bunkmates. Attention.

Gaby wasn't normally one to hold her tongue, and at any other time she would have let Chelsea know exactly what she was thinking. But things were different at Camp Lakeview this year. Not many girls had come back, and Dr. Steve seemed to think it was because Gaby and her friends were "cliquey" and fought too much. That, combined with the totally freaky time they'd had on their overnight (which had gotten weird in just about every way possible, not just where Chelsea was concerned), had led bunk 5A to decide it was time to get along no matter what. Gaby couldn't say anything to Chelsea – she would just end up getting branded as "The Mean Girl".

"Hey," Gaby said, hoping to channel her annoyance into something useful. "Now that we're all rested up, you know what would be fun?"

Priya, who'd been lying back in her rubber ring, half asleep, opened one eye. "What, Gaby?"

Gaby smiled encouragingly. "A relay race. Right?"

Slowly, the rest of her bunkmates roused from their relaxation. Gaby could tell from their grumbling that they weren't entirely sold.

"A *race*?" asked Chelsea. "I dunno."

"I'm not in my *athletic* mode," Nat announced in a sleepy voice. "I'm in my *meditation* mode. Changing modes is really difficult."

"Come *on*," Gaby coaxed. She turned to the athletes in the group, the ones she knew would love her idea. "Jenna and Alex, don't you think a race would be fun? We should get some exercise while we're out here. We can't just turn into, like, lake potatoes."

Alex started to smile. "Good point," she said. "A race *totally* sounds fun. I'll be a team captain!"

"Me too," added Jenna.

Gaby pushed off her ring and stood up in the waist-high water. "Guys, it was my idea, so I think *I* should be a team captain," she said cheerfully. This was a great idea — she'd get to lead her team to victory, and everyone would be psyched up. Gaby knew that some of the girls thought she could be bossy or harsh, but she also knew she was a great leader — and the more she could let her friends see that side of her, the better. "And the other captain should be..." Gaby turned to face her bunkmates and grinned. Half of them — the ones who didn't want to have the race in the first place — looked bored. But the *other* half were smiling, nodding, trying to catch Gaby's eye so she would pick them. Gaby decided to be nice. "Chelsea."

Chelsea grinned, looking surprised and pleased, and got off her ring. Pretty soon everyone was doing the same, and they all swam back to the dock to dump their rings there.

"All right, let's choose our teams. Alex," Gaby called.

"Jenna," Chelsea replied.

"Val."

"Priya."

Pretty soon the bunk was split between the two teams, and even the girls who hadn't really wanted to race seemed to be getting into it. Gaby chose the course of the race.

"Each person swims from here to the raft and back, then tags the next person," she announced. "No skipping turns. You have to hit the raft. And once we start, we don't stop *for any reason.*" She tried to look each bunkmate in the eye as she surveyed the crowd. "Got it?"

"Got it," agreed Jenna shortly. "Can we start now?"

"Yeah." Brynn, who'd ended up on Chelsea's team with Jenna, smiled. "You're going down! We're gonna crush you!"

"Yeah, *right!*" Alex cried. "You didn't even wanna get off your rubber ring. The *real* athletes are all on this team!"

"What?!" Jenna cried.

"You know what I mean." Alex looked away and tried to shrug.

"Whatever," Chelsea piped up. "At least we're not all busy *meditating*—"

Gaby rushed to interrupt before a fully fledged fight broke out. "Channel that energy into your swimming, ladies! All right. Alex and Jenna swim first. On your mark...get set...*go!*"

"Come on, Jenna!"

"Go get 'em, Alex!"

Priya and Val got into position as Alex and Jenna each slapped the raft and headed back – Alex with a very slight lead over Jenna.

"Come on, come on, come on!" Gaby shouted to Alex. "Keep it moving! We've got to beat Ch – the other team!"

Val took off, followed closely by Priya. Gaby smiled, watching Val gain a small lead. Everything was going perfectly. She'd put herself in the all-important last slot, so that when her team won, *she* would be the one to actually win it for them. Her teammates would be thrilled. Glancing over at Chelsea, she noticed a frown pulling at the corners of her mouth.

Chelsea glanced up just in time to see Gaby watching her. "What are you looking at?" she demanded.

Gaby bristled. She pasted on a fake smile. "Oh, Chelsea," she said, "let's not pick fights with each other. We need peace and quiet, remember?"

Chelsea didn't say anything, but her glare was strong enough to burn holes through Gaby's shirt.

Natalie and Tori were swimming back to the dock now. Natalie swam up to the dock, panting, and tagged Gaby's ankle. Taking a deep breath, Gaby jumped into the lake. She felt the cool water gush over her head, then pushed back up to the surface and started swimming towards the raft.

Gaby wasn't actually that strong a swimmer, but her team already had a nice lead over Chelsea's team. She was halfway to the raft when she heard the *splash* of Chelsea jumping into the lake.

In a few seconds Gaby was at the raft and reached out her hand to slap it. Then she pushed off the raft and started swimming back. She looked back at the dock, expecting to see Chelsea dog-paddling not too far from where she'd just jumped in. But Chelsea was nowhere to be seen. Gaby paused for a second as a horrible thought crossed her mind. *Did she sink or something?* She knew Chelsea wasn't the strongest swimmer, but she'd never thought...

WHACK! SPLASH! Gaby heard someone smacking the raft right behind her, and was suddenly totally soaked by a wave of water. Right before her head went under, she saw a blur of red swim by — *Chelsea's red bathing suit!* Chelsea was now a couple of metres ahead of her, swimming with a fierce determination. *Since when does* Chelsea *swim like that?* Gaby wondered, diving forward to try to catch up. She paddled wildly, really using all of the energy she had this time. *Since you made her mad,* she realized, kicking like crazy. *You provoked Chelsea, and now she's mad enough to want to win. Way to go.*

Gaby tried to ignore everything that was going on around her and just concentrate on catching up to Chelsea's red bathing suit. Soon her lungs were burning, and so were the muscles in her arms and legs.

"Go, Gaby! Come on, come on, come on!"

"You can still win this!"

But no matter what Gaby did, Chelsea remained out in front. Gaby realized that Chelsea was actually a pretty good swimmer when she tried. She just usually didn't. *Smack!* With one fluid motion, Chelsea brought her arm up and tagged the dock, winning the race for her team, who all erupted in cheers. "Way to go, Chelsea!" Jenna yelled. "I guess we showed them who the *real* athletes are."

"Hey, c'mon," called Alex, frowning at her friend. "That's not what I said. I just meant – you know."

"Whatever," Jenna shrugged and looked away. "We won. That's what matters."

Gaby finally reached the dock, panting and totally spent. Her lungs were on fire, and her throat still burned from breathing in water when she'd been submerged by the Chelsea wave. She grabbed the dock and just hung on, looking down into the water, trying to catch her breath.

"Tough luck, Gaby," Chelsea said with a little smile, climbing out of the water and onto the dock. "Maybe try a little harder next time."

To find out what happens next read

REALITY BITES

Out now!

Complete your collection of

SUMMER CAMP
SECRETS

Have you read them all?
Turn over to find out!

Pack the perfect summer accessory
in your beach bag today!

SUMMER CAMP
SECRETS

MISS MANHATTAN
ISBN 9780746084557
City chick Natalie's hiding a big secret from her new friends…

PRANKSTER QUEEN
ISBN 9780746084564
Jenna's practical jokes are out of control. What's bugging her?

BEST FRIENDS?
ISBN 9780746084571
Is Grace's new friend Gaby, from rival bunk 3C, all she seems?

LITTLE MISS NOT-SO-PERFECT
ISBN 9780746084588
Perfect camper Alex can't bear to admit why's she acting so strange.

BLOGGING BUDDIES
ISBN 9780746084601
The camp blog is the perfect place to help out a bunkmate in need…

PARTY TIME!
ISBN 9780746084618
Will the girls still get on at the camp reunion in New York?

THREE'S A CROWD
ISBN 9780746093382
Natalie can't help feeling jealous of super-hip new camper Tori.

WISH YOU WEREN'T HERE
ISBN 9780746093399
Will Sarah's classmate Abby expose Sarah as a geek at camp?

Fancy some more sizzling Summer Camp fun?

✱ Try out Natalie's favourite magazine quizzes and learn how to draw like Alyssa

✱ Discover Jenna's recipes for the best-ever s'mores and Sarah's hottest tips for the most fun things to do on holiday

✱ Get the low-down on all the best bits of Camp Lakeview, from the girls' fave games to tried-and-true campfire songs

✱ Plus, look out for fab competitions, and even get the chance to star on the Summer Camp Secrets website yourself!

It's all at

www.summercampsecrets.co.uk

Check it out now!